She realized that in that instant if there was one thing she wanted as much as to know who she really was, it was Braden.

She ached to feel his hands on her, to feel him inside her, to know what it was like.

"Braden," she said, her voice so thick his name almost didn't come out.

"I feel you," he murmured.

His choice of words at once seemed odd and yet right. He wanted to know her first, but he knew essentially all there was to know about her, the pathetic story of her search for self and place. Maybe part of that search could be answered right now with him. Maybe she was afraid of knowing any more about her past, but she wasn't afraid of this.

To just be a woman at her most basic seemed like the greatest gift on the planet. To stop being guarded, to stop censoring herself, to stop fearing. To just *be*.

* * *

Montana Mavericks: 20 Years in the Saddle!

Dear Reader,

When I wrote the final book for the first Montana Mavericks series over twenty years ago, I had no idea how the series would continue to grow. Coming back to it has been a real adventure for me, and I'm glad I had the chance.

But dealing with my heroine's total amnesia was a whole different kind of challenge. I've never had amnesia, though I've read about and even studied it a bit, but that's not the same as walking in the shoes of someone who is living with it. It required a thought experiment that led me down some fascinating avenues.

What would it be like to awake one day and not remember anything about who you were? Not to have one little smidgeon of a past to guide you or a single person you recognized? How would you cope with not having any of the memories others take for granted? How would you feel about the world and your life? How would it feel not to even know *yourself*?

And I couldn't help but think that amnesia might make you awfully tentative about forming new connections. After all, if you could forget once, you might forget again.

Jennifer faces all these problems and more, but Braden Traub reaches her in a way that won't let her keep her distance. He can't give her back her memory, but he can give her a future worth living for: love.

Enjoy! Happy holidays!

Rachel

A Very Maverick Christmas

—

Rachel Lee

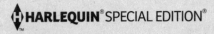
HARLEQUIN® SPECIAL EDITION®

Special thanks and acknowledgment to Rachel Lee for her contribution to the Montana Mavericks: 20 Years in the Saddle! continuity.

Recycling programs
for this product may
not exist in your area.

ISBN-13: 978-0-373-65856-5

A Very Maverick Christmas

Copyright © 2014 by Harlequin Books S.A.

HARLEQUIN®
www.Harlequin.com

Printed in U.S.A.

RACHEL LEE

was hooked on writing by the age of twelve and practiced her craft as she moved from place to place all over the United States. This *New York Times* bestselling author now resides in Florida and has the joy of writing full-time.

To my family, who have blessed me in so many ways.

Chapter One

"I'll meet you there in fifteen minutes," Vanessa said over the phone. "Okay?"

"I'm almost ready," Julie answered, looking around for her boots. "See you." Spying one under the bed, she clicked off the call and made a grab for it.

Going to a Christmas pageant? She wondered if she was losing her mind. All those people... The only thing that was going to be worse was Thanksgiving, right around the corner, a day she was going to spend determinedly by herself.

Trying to feel at home constantly troubled Julie Smith. She had come to Rust Creek Falls nearly six months ago in June, had made a few friends at the Newcomers Club, but she still didn't feel as if she belonged.

But how could she? she wondered as she finished dressing to join her new friends for the Christmas pageant. She had no memory older than four years, and no idea who she was. Julie Smith was a name conveniently tacked to her by the people who had cared for her after the incident that had erased her memory.

But coming out here to Montana to live in this tiny ramshackle cabin sometimes struck her as the ultimate grasping at straws. She looked into the mirror that hung—oddly, she thought—beside her front door and touched the necklace she wore, her only touchstone to her past, gazing at the tarnished coins that hung from it. A specialist in antique coins had told her she was wearing a small fortune around her neck, and that the most recent information he had been able to find about the collection was that it had last been owned by a man in Montana. No name, as collectors preferred to protect their identities, and insurance companies wouldn't give out private information.

So here she was. All because of a necklace and an online blog by someone named Lissa Rourke that had somehow roused a sense of familiarity in her.

Stupid? Maybe. Desperately hunting for a place in this world? Definitely.

For sure, what she found most familiar was the deepening winter. Little enough to cling to.

She smoothed her blue wool sheath over her body and looked at her shoulder-length blond hair. She preferred jeans and Western shirts, and the dress felt awkward. Four years, and she still somehow didn't look right to herself, either. Something was wrong. The hair, she decided, and quickly pulled it back into the ponytail she favored. Better, but the bright blue eyes that stared back at her held no answers to the mystery of who she was. Sometimes she thought she ought to just cut off all her hair, but stopped herself. She'd been able to sell one of her coins, which had given her enough to live on for a while, but that didn't mean she could afford to splurge. Nor did she want to part with another piece of what might be the only clue to her identity.

Sighing, she went to get her coat, wishing she had a longer memory, wishing things in life really seemed to fit somewhere in her experience. But she was woefully inexperienced now. A grown woman with a four-year-old memory. Pathetic. Frustrating.

It struck her, though, as she pulled on her coat, that while Montana was a big state and some conviction that this wasn't the right town kept gnawing at her, things did strike her as familiar. Cowboys. Horses. Even the occasional family name. Those small familiarities kept her here, kept her hoping.

She felt more at home here, if she could feel that at all, than she had at any time since her memory loss.

But what was home? She didn't even know. And if she ever found out who she really was, could she be sure she would feel that other woman was really her? Or would she meet a stranger inside her own head?

Stop it, she told herself. Time to look forward to whatever tonight would bring, and stop peering backward into a black hole.

It had been hard enough to join the Newcomers Club. She suspected she hadn't always been so uncomfortable with people, but how would she know? Going to the pageant tonight had taken some persuasion from her small group of friends. Big groups still overwhelmed her, mainly because she felt out of context. Always out of context and unsure how to react. She didn't have a list of anecdotes to tell about herself in casual conversation, and much of her experience since the amnesia was off-limits. She couldn't bring herself to expose that flaw to anyone.

So she kept quiet, tentatively reacting, speaking only rarely about the most recent events around here, and that left her little enough confidence or conversation. Somehow she had to build enough of a future to have a past.

Because she suspected she might never regain her full memory. As time passed, it became less likely. But maybe she could find at least some snatches of who she had once been.

Maybe someday she'd feel less like she'd been born spontaneously into adulthood.

Headlights flared through the window of the tiny, two-room cabin she rented on the outskirts of town, casting the battered furnishings briefly in harsh light. Her new friends were here.

All she had to do was take one step at a time. Minute by minute, she just had to forge ahead.

It sounded easier than it was. She touched her necklace again before buttoning her coat. It was the only good luck in her new life and her only proof of her past.

Sitting near the front in the auditorium, near Mallory Franklin and her fiancé, Caleb Dalton, Vanessa Brent and Cecelia Clifton, Julie felt mostly uninterested in the show. It was a typical Christmas pageant, although she had no idea how she knew that. But then Mallory's niece, Lily, entered garbed as a darling angel, and the world seemed to stop for Julie.

All of a sudden she had a flash of wearing a similar costume, mouthing similar lines. Then, in an instant, the vision was gone.

She felt herself tremble as she came back to the crowded room, and wondered if she'd had a flash of real memory. Could she have ever played an angel in a Christmas pageant? Soon she realized that the people around her were applauding, and she halfheartedly joined in, trying to paste a smile to her face.

As the applause died away, and everyone waited for the show's little actors to emerge from backstage, Vanessa started talking. She was a tall, lovely woman with curly brown hair and sparkling eyes that for some reason Julie couldn't help but envy.

"I always love Christmastime," Vanessa said. "Don't you, Julie?"

"It's beautiful," Julie answered cautiously. She couldn't understand her reaction to little Lily's angel outfit, or why she still felt shaken.

"We used to have this family tradition," Vanessa continued. "I think I'm going to start it with my family." Over Halloween, Vanessa had gotten engaged to architect Jonah Dalton, and she clearly couldn't wait to begin their new life together.

"What's that?" Julie asked.

"Everyone—siblings, parents, cousins—got holiday pajamas exactly alike. Then on Christmas Eve we'd all gather on the staircase and take a group photo."

"Ooh, I like that," Cecelia said. She tossed her dark hair back over her shoulders. "Mind if I steal it?"

"Help yourself, if you can find the pajamas." Vanessa giggled. "It wasn't always easy."

Mallory spoke. Beside Vanessa she appeared especially petite. She looked ready to jump up from her chair the instant her niece, Lily, appeared. "I think my tradition for a while is going to be making costumes for Lily. She loved this whole pageant idea. But as for family traditions, oh, we had loads. From who did which job decorating the tree to the foods we had for dinner." She smiled at Julie. "What about you?"

"I…" There it was again. Just the big blank that held her back from being a part of all this. "I just loved the season no matter how we celebrated."

"No traditions?"

Julie had to fight an urge to flee. She hadn't told anyone in this town about her amnesia, and this wasn't the place to start. "None that stuck." At least not stuck to her memory.

"Maybe you can start your own," Mallory said, then jumped up and grabbed Julie's arm. "There's Lily. Let's go tell her how wonderful she was." Caleb had already moved toward his soon-to-be daughter. Julie was touched by his eagerness to reach the girl. She wondered what it must have been like to be loved like that…but she couldn't remember.

Lily was a perfect little doll with a mouth that often embarrassed her aunt. She'd been adopted from China by Mallory's sister, who had died. With long, inky hair and almond eyes, she promised to become a stunning beauty.

Except for that costume. Something about it made Julie hesitant to approach. Mallory just kept tugging her closer, and she forced herself to don a smile and get ready to congratulate the little girl.

The Traubs and Daltons were already gathered, telling Lily how beautifully she had done. Julie had already met some of the Daltons through Mallory, but the Traubs were still utter strangers to her. As they approached, Vanessa suddenly poked her gently in the ribs. "Look at who showed up."

"Who?" Julie asked blankly.

"Braden Traub. The last single Traub brother. He's gorgeous enough that I might have given him a second look except I met Jonah. I hear the whole family gives him a hard time about still being a bachelor. Anyway, I guess he managed to come in from the ranch for once."

"But you got Jonah Dalton," Julie said with passable cheer. "Complaints?"

"Absolutely none. I just wish he could be here. Nick, too. You should hear Cecelia complain about her loneliness. The guys are working too hard right now."

"Needs must." Julie attempted to sound light, but she

knew all about loneliness, she figured. She had no one at all. How nice it must be to have someone to miss.

Julie, who, unlike many of the women she had met at the club, hadn't come to Rust Creek looking for the cowboy of her dreams, finally picked out Braden from his family. They all shared similar good looks, but Vanessa was right. He was drop-dead gorgeous.

Apparently, amnesia hadn't deprived her of the ability to feel a quiver of response to a handsome, muscular man with brown hair and eyes that seemed to hold a sparkle. She'd been putting her sexuality on the back burner since her amnesia, for good reason. Her sudden reaction to Braden was almost disheartening. If she didn't know herself, she shouldn't even consider such things. No guy would want her in this condition anyway.

They reached Lily at last, and Julie squatted before the child to tell her how wonderful she'd been. Then before she could stop the words, she said, "When I was five I got to be the angel, too. I was so scared." Where had that come from?

"I wasn't," Lily answered confidently. "It was lots of fun." She beamed at the gathered adults, who all smiled and laughed. As soon as Julie straightened, Lily, clearly feeling like a queen bee at the moment, introduced her to everyone, Traubs and Daltons both, including little Noelle. They plunged into a discussion of past Christmas events, clearly trying to include her in a neighborly way.

Wondering how she could talk about something she didn't really remember, Julie started looking for a graceful escape. She could wait outside until Vanessa was ready to go.

Before she could take a step, Lily spoke again, freezing her. "Julie? I think you should talk to Braden. He hasn't got anybody yet, either."

Mallory gasped. "Lily! I've told you to stop saying embarrassing things to people."

Julie looked down in time to see the girl's face fall into a frown.

"Making friends is good. What's embarrassing?" Lily asked.

Plenty, Julie thought, wanting to sink through the floor.

But Braden pretended nothing had happened. His brother Dallas spoke. "About time you met the recluse, Julie. The last of the living Traub bachelors."

Braden offered his hand with a smile, and Julie reluctantly took it. His palm felt warm and callused, but it had more of an impact than a simple handshake should. Her urge to flee grew. She couldn't risk wanting a man, or becoming involved with one. But nothing about him suggested he was feeling anything more than friendly. Oddly enough, given her state of mind, that almost disappointed her.

"Nice to meet you, Julie. Don't listen to Dallas. I'm not a recluse at all."

"No, you just bury yourself in work."

"Only because you guys are so busy romancing the ladies. Or were." Braden released Julie's hand but continued to smile at her. "Why don't you join us at the Triple-T for our after party, and maybe we can get past the Lily-inspired awkwardness."

"What's awk...awkness?" Lily's question dissolved everyone into laughter, breaking any tension that remained.

"Seriously," Braden said. "You don't want to miss the after-show fun. Mallory? How about you and Caleb come, too?"

"I've got to get this little hellion home to bed," Mallory answered. "Sorry to miss out." She turned to Julie. "You really should go. A lot of people will be there, and it's always a great time. Vanessa can take you, or I can drop you to get your own car."

"I'll think about it," Julie said, while firmly convinced that she was going to bolt. Then she met Braden's friendly gaze again. Or maybe not.

She had apparently recovered a memory tonight. Maybe getting out more into larger groups would jar something loose.

With her heart in her throat, she agreed to go. But only for a short visit, she promised herself.

Braden knew his brothers were going to rib him about inviting Julie to the Triple-T, but he was so used to being ribbed about his dating life—or lack thereof—that he really didn't care. He'd dated before, he'd date again when the time was right. Just now it didn't feel right.

But something about Julie Smith had managed to reach out to him. For some weird reason, she made him feel like she needed a protector. Yeah, she was beautiful all right, but with an aura of innocence that cried out for shelter. And something else, something uneasy. Julie Smith was not a truly happy young woman, and that affected him.

She touched him, striking some kind of responsive chord, and it wasn't just those huge blue eyes, her soft face, her great figure. Those things were just a package, and at thirty-four, Braden wasn't often deceived by the packaging. He'd managed to learn a few lessons over the years.

But he'd always been a sucker for someone or something that needed protecting, whether a friend or a new foal. He could be all wrong about her, but he supposed he'd figure that out quickly.

At first he left her pretty much alone among the family and friends at the Triple-T. A party was underway, and he was one of the hosts. But he kept seeking her out with his eyes, and every time he noticed how uncomfortable she looked. The folks in his home were all friendly, but apparently, as a newcomer, she felt awkward. In fact, she looked as if she wished she could melt into the walls. He was sure people weren't trying to ignore her or make her feel out of place. Instead, she seemed to be creating her own bubble, emerging only when she had to so she could return a greeting or shake a hand. Welcomed but not feeling it.

His curiosity about her began to grow. She was definitely *not* just another one of the women who had showed up here hoping to find a husband as they rebuilt the town after the flood. Not to say all those women were bad or anything. But this one seemed to be looking for escape more than company.

Curiosity might be his worst failing, he thought with some amusement as he realized he was steadily circling through the room toward her. He just loved a mystery.

He amused himself even more because he'd seen this woman around town a few times but had never felt the least urge to meet her, until tonight. Ah yes, mystery. Well, he'd try to find out what it was, kill his curiosity and move on. Things were too hectic on the ranch with all his brothers distracted by their families and girlfriends for him to spare the time for much more anyway.

He saw his parents get to her first. It was mostly a family party, and apparently they didn't want her to feel like a loose end. As he drew nearer, he heard them greeting her as if she were some kind of celebrity guest, glad she had taken the time to join them, hoping she would visit often. They even threw in a little matchmaking of their own, extolling Braden's virtues.

And Julie, whether they knew it or not, was beginning to look almost frightened. What the hell?

His parents moved on finally, and he prepared to step in. Whatever was going on, he didn't want her scared.

She started to walk around the room, looking at family pictures on the dark wood wall. His opening, if he could catch up to her. He didn't miss the fact that she was drawing ever closer to Vanessa, who was her escape route.

He quickened his step and caught her finally as she stopped to look up at the portrait of his grandfather.

"My grandfather," he said to her.

She started, then looked at him with those huge blue eyes. "You have a big family."

"Yeah. When I was a kid, I sometimes wished I was an only child. Now everyone's moved out with their new families and when I stay here, I sometimes feel like I'm rattling around in this place."

She gave a tentative laugh.

"What about you?" he asked. "Large family?"

"Only child."

The brevity of her response invited no more questions, but he was determined. "Parents?"

"Gone."

God, he thought, that was sad. She was truly alone. Friends couldn't make up for the absence of family, something he'd learned as his brothers moved out to be with their brides and girlfriends. "I'm sorry."

Just then Dallas appeared at his side, having left his wife Nina to talk to their mother, and bumped his shoulder. "Coon dog smelling possum?" he asked.

"Damn it, Dallas." Some women wouldn't appreciate that kind of rough humor. "Go back to your wife and lay off."

Dallas simply grinned.

Braden glared at him then turned to apologize to Julie. Too late. In just those few moments, she'd managed to reach Vanessa. The two women were talking, and Vanessa nodded. They were leaving.

"Strike out?" Dallas asked.

"I'll never know, you big idiot. You scared her off."

"Looked to me like you were doing a pretty good job of that yourself."

Braden paused. Had he been?

His instinct told him to go to the door to say goodnight, but Dallas's words held him back. That woman didn't need any more scaring. Instead, he watched as his parents bade the women good-night and made them promise to come back again soon.

"Damn it," he said again.

"You can always invite her to help at Presents for Patriots. Innocent enough."

"I don't need your advice."

"Wanna bet?" Dallas asked.

Braden realized the room had nearly emptied. It looked even emptier with most of the furniture moved back against the walls to make room. The gals had apparently gone to the kitchen to help with cleanup. That left the merciless crew of Sutter, Dallas, and Collin to stand around with him, converging like vultures who spied a meal. They'd tussled and teased with each other since their earliest days, and Braden didn't need a map to know what he was in for now. He'd actually talked to a single woman.

"Brother Braden," Sutter said, "has the hots for a cute little blonde."

It was hopeless, but Braden argued anyway. Silence might only make it worse. "I was just trying to make her feel welcome here. I said maybe a half dozen words to her."

"Yeah, but it was all about what was in your eyes," Collin retorted.

"Since when did you read eyes?"

Dallas snorted a laugh. "Since you started broadcasting. About time you looked at a woman that way. Stuck here all by yourself as a bachelor. Mom and Dad are worried."

"Mom and Dad are less worried than you four. What is it about people who get married? They want everyone to join them? Doesn't matter if you're happy or not?"

"You don't know if you'd be happy," Clay remarked. "You never stuck with anyone long enough."

"Because I wasn't happy."

"I think you should go for that woman," Dallas opined. "Get on your horse and ride over to her place and make her swoon at the sight of a real cowboy."

Braden reached for a throw pillow from one of the couches and threw it at him. "I don't think she's in the market for a cowboy. Besides, I'm not in the market, either. Now will you just lay off? I was trying to be courteous."

Of course it didn't end there. It never did. His brothers continued to razz him until the his mom and the growing crowd of his sisters-in-law and soon-to-be sisters-in-law reappeared. He took a few more verbal jabs, but the presence of the ladies toned them down.

And that, thought Braden, was a good reason not to get involved with a woman. Next thing you knew, you'd be leaving your boots outside the door and turning all proper-like.

That was just an excuse and he knew it. His brothers changed a bit around their ladies because with them they could show a different side, a gentler side, than they did with each other.

A good thing, he supposed. But sometimes he really did feel like the odd man out, now that they'd all found their mates. Hell, he was the last man standing. The thought brought a wry smile to his lips.

But he was sure his interest in Julie Smith had entirely to do with the aura of mystery around her and nothing to do with how pretty she was. He almost asked if anyone knew anything about her, but stopped himself just in time.

He could take the razzing, but right now he didn't feel like taking it about Julie. She'd reached some place inside him that he didn't want anyone else to touch.

Some dangerously protective place, which meant keeping his brothers out of this as much as possible. More remarks like the one Dallas had made tonight, and Julie Smith might vanish from town as suddenly as she had arrived.

Later, though, in a quiet moment as he was getting ready to sleep in his old bedroom rather than head over to his own place, his mother spoke to him.

"Braden?"

"Yeah?" He had one foot in the doorway of his bedroom.

"That Julie Smith."

He tensed. "Mom…"

"Just listen to me. She's very pretty and seems very nice. I know Vanessa, Mallory and Cecelia all like her. But no one knows anything about her, really. So, while I'd like to see you settled and happy…"

He looked into the face that had loved him since birth and turned to give her a big hug. "I'll be careful, Mom. I always have been, much to your disappointment."

Ellie Traub laughed. "Maybe. I'm surprised she hasn't dated while she's been here. And it's not for want of guys asking, I believe."

"She's a wounded bird, Mom. That's all. I just want to know what's going on."

Ellie's smile faded. "That's dangerous, Braden."

"I know."

"Just be careful. If I'd known how you were going to turn out, I'd probably have named you Parsival."

"Thank God you didn't." He laughed. "I'm no knight errant on a quest, just a frustrated detective."

"I hope you're right." She put a hand on his shoulder and drew him close for a kiss on his cheek. "Good night, my boy."

He watched her disappear toward her room then entered his own and closed the door. The woman who'd earlier been acting as if the answer to her prayers had arrived that night was now cautioning him.

He didn't miss her point. Not at all.

Chapter Two

For the next few days, Julie felt as if the inside of her head had become a huge jumble. Her memory, if that's what it was, of being an angel in a Christmas pageant when she was young, was really niggling her.

She pulled up that flash over and over, trying to wring every possible detail out of it that she could. Standing on stage, wings on her back, scanning a sea of faces trying to find her parents and not seeing them.

"Damn," she cussed out loud. If that was a real memory, why couldn't she see her parents?

But even if she had, could she rely on what she thought she remembered? She'd had some counseling since the amnesia, but it had mostly been pithy claims about how she just had to trust her memory, such as it was, and perhaps her past would return to her.

Trust it? She couldn't even be sure it was a true memory. It might have been some kind of daydream, resulting from a desperate need to fill in the huge hole her past had become.

But maybe, just maybe, there was some link in her head with the holidays. She should make more of an effort to enjoy the season as it ramped up. Maybe it would jar some more memories loose for her. Maybe little shards would grow into big pieces.

But somehow, one little girl in an angel costume had

managed to throw her entire being into some kind of blender. Conviction and doubt warred within her, alongside hope and despair.

Then there was Braden Traub. She told herself he'd just been being nice to her, but he might as well have warning flags all over him. For the first time since she lost her memory, she felt attracted to a man. Seriously attracted. Forgotten urges had wakened in an instant. Dangerous, because she had no memory. She was sure that the instant a guy found out she was amnesiac, he'd head for the hills. But apart from that, she was a babe in the woods. No memory to guide her about dealing with men. About dating.

Hell, she couldn't even carry on much of a conversation unless it was about the last few months. So why take a risk?

She sighed and rubbed her aching head. Again and again she had been warned about trying to force her memory, but she kept trying anyway. Desperation gnawed at her.

Like looking at those family portraits at the Triple-T. She'd hoped one of them would jog her in some way, but none of them had. Instead, all they had done was make her feel even lonelier. She didn't even have one photo tied to her past.

But then, she didn't even know what had happened to her. The doctors theorized she might have been mugged or had an accident, but she'd been found wandering with nothing to show for her experience except a cracked skull and no memory. And her necklace. Her talisman.

And a desire for cold and snow that had led her to New England, where she'd met the man who had researched her necklace and told her the last owner had lived in Montana. Then she'd come across that blog and felt drawn here like a homing pigeon.

But what did any of that mean? Again, she was without context. In some ways that was the most frustrating thing of all: urges and impulses that drove her without having any idea why.

If she couldn't explain herself to herself, how could she explain herself to anyone?

When she realized she was thoroughly cleaning the cabin again for the third time in as many days, she stopped and tried to give herself a wake-up call.

One of the two rooms she was working so hard on was a bathroom. Otherwise the cabin contained a larger room that held a small kitchen at one corner, an alcove beside the bathroom where she had a bed, and a beastly woodstove that terrified her because she'd never had to use one before, at least not that she could remember. As winter deepened, she prayed the power would stay on, because if it didn't the heater wouldn't work and she was going to get very cold. Maybe she should buy a kerosene space heater, although those were dangerous, too.

Sighing, she rubbed her temples. For three days she hadn't gone out her front door, not since the party at the Triple-T. What was with her? The town was familiar enough now that she felt all right when she walked the streets and shopped. The woods around the cabin were like a personal cathedral for her, offering peace and serenity. So what was she doing being a hermit?

She stuffed her feet into her warm winter boots and pulled her parka off the peg. A bracing walk would do her good, clearing out cobwebs and probably settling her frantic ramblings. The winter snow was not yet deep, although she had been warned that it would get there soon enough. For now, though, she could walk in the woods or into town.

She locked up the cabin behind her, then hesitated on the stoop. The woods or town? She needed a few things from the grocery, and increasingly she had a desire to find some splash of color to add to the cabin. The inside of it was almost dismal; age had faded everything so much. A throw pillow or two, or maybe just a small throw she could wrap herself in when it became drafty. The bedding was her only addition, and sadly she'd chosen a wintry look that right now didn't help at all.

Why did winter call to her anyway? What she needed as the days grew shorter, colder and darker, were some really bright colors.

God, she couldn't even bring herself to put a mark on the place where she lived. She seemed to spend all her time feeling as if she might have to bolt at any moment, a purely ridiculous idea. Certainly no one had made her feel that way.

She figured she'd winter in this town then perhaps move on again if she unlocked nothing about herself. That, she thought, was her real problem: trying on places and people, then hitting the road to search for the key to her memory.

But how could she put down roots? She had two huge fears: that she might plant herself in the wrong place and thus lose any chance of finding out who she was, and that she'd find out and not like what she learned. Given that those were polar opposites, she sometimes wondered what the heck she was doing.

She turned toward the woods then changed her mind. If nothing else, she could bring at least one piece of cheer into that cabin. Maybe something Christmasy, given her reaction to Lily's costume. Maybe Christmas held some kind of key for her.

She'd bought a battered, secondhand car with some of the money she'd received for the sale of her coin, and she climbed into the blue monster now in case the day turned colder, or in case she actually splurged on something besides a few groceries. A Christmas tree? But then she'd have to decorate it.

Shaking her head at her own indecision, she turned over the ignition. This heap might not look like much, but it had turned out to be amazingly reliable so far. Probably the good thing about buying locally. The garage owner had a reputation to maintain in a relatively small town.

She was driving up Cedar toward the Crawford General Store when she spied that psychic Winona Cobbs, her white hair flying in the breeze. That woman made Julie uneasy, although she wasn't sure exactly why. When Winona had given a talk back in August about listening to inner voices, she'd seemed slightly dotty but not crazy. Afterward, as Julie had been drawn forward to meet the woman, she had felt an almost electric zap. In that instant Winona had snapped her head around, looked at her then shrugged and returned to her conversation.

Whatever it was that had happened, Julie had no desire to repeat the experience. It had been weird, even creepy.

On a weekday morning, finding parking near the General Store was easy. Julie slid into a spot then pondered exactly what she intended to do there. Most folks here drove to Kalispell for major shopping, but the General Store had a bit of everything. She could not only get a few chicken breasts and veggies for dinner the next few nights, but she could also wander through a miserly selection of Western clothing and even some decorator items. She was almost positive she could find a pillow and a throw in here, although she'd have a bigger selection in Kalispell.

That didn't entice her to pull out. Small things that mattered very little weren't enough to drag her to a bigger town. Her needs, both psychological and physical, could be met here.

At least until she decided she needed to move on again.

Shaking her head at herself, she climbed out and headed into the store. Although it hadn't been destroyed in the flood last year, some repairs had obviously been necessary regardless, because the store had clearly been freshly painted not that long ago. It was certainly jammed with merchandise. The Crawford family was doing their best to give people a reason to shop locally.

She didn't get two steps inside the door before she was greeted by Nina Crawford Traub.

"Nice to see you, Julie. Can I help you find something?"

"Groceries, eventually, but I'm looking for a little color to add to my place."

"I can help with that," Nina said cheerfully. "Got a whole bunch of new Christmas stuff in."

Which would be useless in little more than a month, Julie thought as she followed Nina. On the other hand, she *was* wondering if Christmas might hold some kind of key for her.

Nina finally waved her hand expansively at an area clearly marked out for the holiday season. Thanksgiving items were marked down as the big day was nearly upon them. Christmas colors shrieked from a heaped table and some nearby racks.

"Christmas tree decorations are in the back." Nina pointed to her right, then her left. "If you want nonseasonal, look over there. Call if you need me."

A pretty impressive display for such a relatively small space, Julie thought as she began to wander around the table. Stockings, pillows, tree skirts, even some holiday-themed costume jewelry. Someone had tried to hit every possibility, including a basket of inexpensive stocking stuffers.

But nothing struck her. Nothing touched her. Nothing seemed to jar anything within her. Well, if she was going to spend any money at all on brightening the place, she guessed the nonseasonal area would be the place to look.

She was just fingering a bright blue throw, almost electric in its brilliance, when a familiar voice caused her to freeze.

"Hi," said Braden Traub. Then when she didn't immediately answer, "I'm sorry. I didn't mean to intrude."

Suddenly galvanized, embarrassed by what might appear to be rudeness, she turned and saw him half smiling at her. "You're not," she blurted, once again struck by how attractive he was. He wore a shearling jacket with gloves hanging out of the pockets, jeans and boots. An iconic man most women would drool over. She hoped she avoided that embarrassment.

"I tore up a couple of shirts over the last week," he said casually as if he didn't mind starting a conversation in the middle. "Damn barbed wire. So I'm replacing them. That's a pretty color you're looking at there."

She glanced at the soft wool fabric between her fingers. "Yes, it is." Then she made an effort. "I need to brighten my place up a little."

"You're at the old cabin outside town, right?"

"Yes."

"It needs brightening," he agreed. "I haven't been in there for a few years, but it needed some back then, too."

"Um…"

"Yes?" he said encouragingly.

"How could you tear shirts on barbed wire? Did it cut through your jacket?"

His smile widened. "No jacket. I was dealing with some rolls in the barn and got careless. I'm lucky I didn't need stitches."

"Shirts might cost almost as much." It pleased her immensely when he laughed.

"There is that," he agreed. "And the fact that I was careless more than once. I ought to know better."

"I hope they were old shirts."

"On their last legs. Are you thinking about decorating for Christmas? I could help you get a tree to your place."

She blinked. A man whose own brothers claimed he was a recluse was offering to help her get a tree and bring it to her cabin? Then it struck her they might have been joking. "You and your brothers joke a lot."

Surprise widened his dark eyes a bit, then he laughed again as he apparently caught her reference. "Oh, you mean what Dallas said about me being a recluse. Yeah, we joke a lot. The teasing is merciless. That's the only thing I don't mind about them all being at their own places now. It's so dang peaceful."

She felt a smile begin to dawn on her own face. "Things can be too peaceful."

"Well, sometimes, but they come back often enough to keep me on my toes. I think they'll all calm down when they have their own little Noelles."

"That's your niece? She's so cute."

"I think so, but I'm biased. Well, let me know if you need help with anything. I'm going to be in town for a few hours." He started to turn away then paused. "Are you coming to the church to help with gift wrapping for the troops?"

"I've already promised Vanessa I will."

"Great. See you there." Then he paused again. "Unless you'd like to get some coffee when you're done here?"

The invitation completely startled her. She'd been asked out a few times since she arrived here and had turned down all the offers. But it felt different to be casually asked for coffee. Part of her wanted to flee, because it was so tiring to conceal all the gaps in her memory, but another part of her wanted to keep looking at him, listening to him.

Becoming a hermit, she told herself sternly, wasn't going to do the least thing to solve her problem. In fact, it might hinder her.

"I'd love coffee," she answered, hoping her hesitation hadn't been too noticeable.

"Great!" His smile widened again. "How long do you need?"

"Well, I have to pick out…" She stopped herself. Delaying tactics weren't going to help anything. "I need to grab some groceries. Nothing that won't keep in the car for a while. Twenty minutes?"

"Twenty minutes. Just enough time for me to pick and pay for my shirts. See you at checkout."

She envied him his easiness, his ability to seem comfortable in his own skin. She often hoped she didn't look as skittish and frightened as she sometimes felt.

On impulse, she grabbed the electric-blue throw and a couple of red, glittery Christmas pillows, both with angels on them. Cost be hanged, she thought as she headed over to the groceries. Color seemed imperative now, and it was apt to get more so as the winter deepened and darkened.

Coffee with the mystery lady, Braden thought, feeling as if he'd just made a huge leap. Of course, if anyone saw him having coffee with Julie Smith, the teasing was going to go through the roof.

Oh, well. He was used to it. Being the last Traub bachelor in town had not only increased the teasing, but had taught him that he seemed to be under some kind of local microscope, too. All the women who had come into town in a veritable wave looking for husbands had added to the local curiosity about a guy who seemed impervious to all those wiles.

He could just imagine what some folk suspected, although he didn't really care. When the right woman came along, well… It was as his mother had once said, "Dating is a series of no, no, no until you finally get to yes." Well, he'd had a few nos, enough to realize that dating could be a huge investment. Better to be picky before you really got started.

He pulled four plain Western shirts off the rack, glad that he hadn't given in to a whim to go to Kalispell for a few hours. All he'd wanted were work shirts, and now he was going to have coffee with Julie Smith. His curiosity quickened again. At the very least he wanted to know why such a beautiful young woman seemed to hang back in some very noticeable ways.

Sort of like him, he thought humorously. Maybe she had some bad romances in her past.

"Stocking up again," said Nina as she checked him out. "You're hard on shirts, Braden Traub. Dallas takes better care than you do."

"Blame it on the barbed wire."

Nina rolled her eyes. Once his shirts were in a paper bag, he saw Julie approaching with a cart that contained two red throw pillows, the electric-blue blanket she'd been admiring, and some packaged chicken breasts, frozen vegetables and a couple of potatoes.

Bachelor fare, he thought as he stood back and waited. And given how cold it was outside, sunshine notwithstanding, if she put everything in her trunk, it would probably freeze before she got home.

Assuming he could keep her from bolting before she'd spent ten minutes with him.

God, she was pretty. Each time he looked at her, he felt it anew. And it wasn't just those big blue eyes, blond hair or figure. It was an aura of, well, innocence. She reminded him of a lamb exploring the world for the first time, trying bravely and then showing huge timidity at something startlingly new. But she had to be somewhere in her early twenties, and that didn't seem to fit with the whole innocence thing. More innocent than he was, certainly, but not a child.

He hoped he'd find out something about her. If he could quiet his curiosity, maybe he wouldn't feel so drawn to her, and he could safely escape another entanglement doomed for failure.

He offered to help with her bags, although he was sure she could have carried them herself. Manners had been ingrained at an early age. A kind of old-fashioned chivalry, judging by much of what he saw of the world today. He had no doubt, however, that Nina would report back to Dallas, and he'd take another round of ribbing. Sometimes this town could be too small.

She blushed, but let him take a couple of the bags and carry them to her car. Then she lowered the boom he'd half expected.

"I should get this food home and into a refrigerator."

Braden didn't often give anyone a hard time, but some stubbornness reared in him. "It's freezing out here. You put the chicken and frozen vegetables in your trunk, and it'll stay colder than it would in your fridge while we have coffee. Not the potatoes, though. Don't want them to freeze."

In the bright morning sunlight, with the air as clear as fresh-washed glass, she looked even prettier. He saw emotions chase across her face, and she bit her lip.

"It's just coffee," he said gently.

"Just coffee," she repeated. Then, at long last, "Okay."

"Let's go to Daisy's donut shop on North Broomtail," he prodded gently. "You can bring your own car and run as soon as you need to."

Her face darkened in a way that told him he'd said exactly the wrong thing, but then, making an effort, she smoothed it over. "Sure. I'll see you there."

Wondering if she'd even show up, he went over to his mud-splashed truck, climbed in and left it to her to follow. He wasn't going to force himself on any woman, even for a chance to talk.

After Braden drove off, Julie dithered in her car for a few minutes, letting it warm up. Well, that was her excuse anyway. Braden appealed to her, undeniably. She felt a jolt of sexual awareness every time she saw him. But was that enough to take this kind of risk?

What did she have to talk to him about? Her few months here in Rust Creek? His family, whom she did not really know? Maybe she could ask enough questions to keep him talking. But what if he asked questions?

She sat like a terrified rabbit for maybe five minutes until she realized the heat was blasting in her face, and if Braden was waiting for her, she was being rude. He'd helped her load her car. He must be wondering why she hadn't followed right away. That's what any normal woman would have done, wasn't it?

She put the car in gear and headed for the donut shop.

There'd be other people there, limiting their topics of conversation, she assured herself. Besides, as she'd been arguing to herself this morning, being a hermit was unlikely to get her any closer to the answers she wanted.

Stupid, she thought, to so desperately want to know about her past yet be equally frightened of finding out. Normal reaction, the psychologist had said, but how could anyone really know what was normal for someone who'd lost all memory of her past until she woke in a hospital unable to even remember her name? Her kind of retrograde amnesia was extremely rare, so rare that at first the doctors hadn't seemed to believe her.

Some memory loss happened. Total memory loss was in a class of its own, evidently.

It didn't take long to reach the donut shop. Braden's truck was there, and she glimpsed him through the window. He waved when he saw her pulling in. The gesture warmed her a bit, and took the edge off her nerves. At least her knees didn't feel like rubber as she climbed out and walked toward the door. She'd get through this, the way she had gotten through everything so far.

She had certainly gotten through a lot. Her memory of the last four years, short though it was, reminded her that she was made of sterner stuff than she sometimes thought. Maybe she should congratulate herself on getting this far, instead of fearing the next twenty minutes.

But his remark about her being able to run as soon as she wanted returned to her, and she wondered if she was giving everyone the impression that she wanted to bolt. Well, sometimes she did. Sometimes she seriously wanted to bolt from this whole situation. But where could she go? This was one of those things she would take with her wherever she went. No escape.

To her surprise, Braden opened the door for her. She

hadn't expected that, just walking into a coffee shop. His smile was welcoming, his voice kind as he teased, "I thought I'd lost you."

His eyes were warm, just like his smile, and she felt some inner tension let go. "I just warmed up the car a bit. The guy I bought it from said I shouldn't make a habit of running with a cold engine."

"Good advice, usually. You can see how well I pay attention to it."

He motioned her to the booth, and she loosened her coat.

Braden remained on his feet until she slid into the bench facing where he'd been sitting. Only then did he sit facing her. "I'm going to have a latte," he said. "Don't let anybody know. I'll be hearing from my brothers how I need to drink *real* coffee. The manly stuff."

More of her tension seeped away, and she laughed. "Grow-hair-on-your-chest coffee, huh?"

"Something like that, although that day is long past. Did you ever wonder why they tell you coffee will stunt your growth when you're young, and then when you get older it'll make you manly?"

She laughed again. "No, sorry. Wrong gender."

His head tipped a little, a laugh escaped him, then he leaned toward her a bit, his eyes dancing. "The things your gender has spared you. What will you have? My treat, and the sky's the limit."

She looked up at the menu hanging over the counter. "I'll have the mocha cinnamon latte," she decided, then nearly patted her own back for finding it so easy to order. So natural. Some things didn't feel at all natural to her anymore. So maybe her previous self had liked that kind of coffee?

Pointless question.

Braden called the waitress over. "Candy? When you have a sec?"

She returned her attention to Braden as he ordered for them, adding a couple of blueberry muffins. "I hope you like them," he said to her as the waitress walked away.

"I do," she admitted. Then a thought occurred to her. He'd called the waitress by name. "Do you know everyone in town?"

"Certainly not you," he said lightly. Then more seriously, "No, I don't know everyone. We've had a lot of new people come to help with the floods and other things."

"And you're very busy at the ranch?" Keep asking questions, don't give him a chance to pry.

"These days, yes. My brothers are busy with their personal lives. They have their own businesses and families to take care of these days. Can't say I blame them."

Her smile came easily. "Me neither. Which is how you came to be wrestling with barbed wire?"

He grinned. "Exactly. And wrestling is a good term for it. Are you ready for our winter?"

The change of subject seemed abrupt, but at least she could answer truthfully. "I love winter."

"Maybe not winters here so much. We get dang cold. Where'd you come from?"

"New England." Which was truthful insofar as it went. "Part of what drew me out here was the idea of snow-capped mountains. Real mountains. And Lissa Roarke's blog, of course. Though I gather she's now Lissa Christensen." Julie had learned from local gossip that Lissa had married her own Rust Creek cowboy, Sheriff Gage Christensen, a few months after her arrival in town last year.

"I never had much time to read her blog," he said, leaning back as the waitress, Candy, served them. He thanked her. "I hope she didn't make us seem overly romantic."

"Depends on what you mean by romance. I just knew I wanted mountains and snow, and this place sounded friendly."

"Do you ski?"

She blinked. A blank wall answered that question. "Not really," she hedged.

"Most people who like snow do. Just asking. I don't have a lot of time for it, myself, but if I can arrange it, I like cross-country. I don't need a slope and don't have to risk permanent disability."

He was cute, she thought, and he made it so easy to laugh. She wanted to keep her guard up, but she was beginning to feel safe with him. For now, at least. Growing warm, she slipped the coat off her shoulders and reached for her coffee.

"Want me to cut the muffins up?" he asked.

"It might make it easier."

Again that twinkle in his eyes. "Depends on who's eating and where." But he unwrapped the flatware that was rolled in the napkin and cut the two muffins into bite-size pieces. Crumbs tumbled all over the plate, but he didn't seem concerned.

"That's an interesting necklace you're wearing," he said, pushing the plate toward her in invitation. "It looks old."

"It is," she admitted. She at least knew something about it for certain. "It's an heirloom." She reached for a piece of muffin and pulled a napkin out of the dispenser to place it on, while she tensed for the next question.

"It's nice to have something like that," he said, picking a piece of muffin for himself. "I like things that pass down through the generations. They create a great sense of connection."

A cowboy philosopher, she thought, and wondered

what he'd think if he knew that necklace was her *only* connection. Probably find an excuse to head back to his ranch and pretend they'd never met.

She picked up her coffee, nearly hiding behind it, wondering why she was so ashamed of her amnesia. It wasn't some kind of personal failing. She'd been severely injured, probably in some awful accident, and should just be grateful to be alive. Why did she feel so embarrassed by it?

Because she wasn't normal. She wasn't anything approaching normal. Missing a limb was more normal than missing your entire past, and most people would probably think she was making it up, or crazy in some way. *That* was the problem. Her dirty little secret.

"I've never experienced winter in New England," he said when he'd swallowed more muffin and coffee. "I wonder how it compares."

"I can't answer. This is my first time here."

Again that devastating grin came to his face. "Maybe we should track the weather this winter and compare the two places. Betcha we get colder."

Remembering the last winter, she felt a smile play around her mouth. "I wouldn't be so sure. We got pretty darn cold last winter. Colder than normal, though." She knew that because she'd heard it countless times.

"Then maybe we beat you in the snow department." When she didn't answer immediately, he winked. "Say, aren't you willing to get into an argument about whose home has the worst winter?"

"You might have better luck with your brothers."

He laughed with pure pleasure. "Good one. Points for you."

She felt her cheeks warm at his approval. Maybe this would become easier.

"You seem thick as thieves with Vanessa."

"She's great. She and Mallory and Cecelia and Callie. They've all been wonderful to me. And I just adore little Lily."

"She's easy to adore, although I suppose I should defend the Traub honor and claim that for Noelle."

"She's adorable, too."

"I just hope she doesn't grow up quite as mouthy as Lily. That girl! Whatever pops into her head comes out of her mouth. I actually like it. Caleb does too except for when it seems to bother Mallory."

"She'll grow out of it. I kind of like knowing where I stand with her."

"Until she tries some matchmaking."

Julie's cheeks flamed. "That *was* a little awkward."

"Actually, it might have been a good idea."

Julie froze. The urge to flee warred with the urge to stand her ground and not look like a fool by running.

"People *do* need friends," he said as if he didn't notice her reaction. Maybe he hadn't. "So, that kind of ended the awkwardness. Then she was so cute when she couldn't say that word."

"She was," Julie said around a thick tongue.

"I guess I shouldn't have brought it up." He looked out the window. "Winona Cobbs keeps saying we're going to get a heckuva blizzard soon. One to remember. I wonder if she's right."

At last, a topic that made Julie feel safe. "Do you believe her predictions? I don't know why, but she makes me a little uneasy."

He returned his attention to her. "We're at the time of year for blizzards. I won't put much stock in a prediction like that unless it flies in the face of meteorology. As for being uneasy around her…well, some folks are. She's essentially a harmless, nice person, but when those eyes settle on you, it's possible to feel like she sees your soul."

Remembering the strange electric tingle she had felt when Winona fixed her gaze on her, Julie could only nod. "There's something about her…"

"Which is why some people listen more than maybe they should. But she means well, I'll give her that. If she's psychic, I don't really know, but she's not cheating widows out of the life insurance, if you get me."

Julie didn't know. She had no memory of psychics. "What do you mean?" she dared to ask.

"Oh, there are some scam artists around who'll charge an arm and a leg to give you some ridiculous reading. Never knew one, just read about them. At least we don't have one of them around here. Winona gets paid for speaking, but never charges for any information she volunteers. To my way of thinking, that makes her honest, even if it doesn't necessarily make her right."

Julie nodded, stuffing some more of the blueberry muffin in her mouth, savoring it then washing it down with her latte. "Great flavor combination," she said after dabbing her lips with a napkin. She didn't want to gossip about local people, even if gossip sometimes seemed to be a favorite pastime. She was willing to listen, but talking was a dangerous thing. There was no way to know, if she said something wrong, whether it would come back to haunt her. And sometimes she feared she simply didn't know what the wrong things to say might be. She seemed to have retained most of her skills from her past, but she couldn't be sure, without memory, how many of them were working right.

"So where in New England are you from?" Braden asked.

At once she tensed, and her mouth started to dry out.

Now would come the questions she couldn't answer because there were no answers. At least she knew the last place she had lived. "Outside Boston, in a town called Worcester."

"I always liked the way that word doesn't sound like it's spelled. I had a terrible time when I was a kid learning to say *Worcestershire*, that sauce. Love it on my steaks. Anyway, mastering that one took long enough that my brothers were merciless. I think I finally got it."

"I'd say so."

"You must be missing your friends."

She felt her face start to freeze. Time to go, before he grew too personal. "I moved a lot," she said finally, glancing at her watch. "And I really need to go."

"So soon?" He studied her. "I said something wrong."

"No, really. I just have some other things I need to do." Like examine her own head, explain to herself why she'd been stupid enough to accept this invitation, even if the guy awoke her entire sexual being. What the hell was she thinking? Yes, she needed to be out more and talk to more people if she was ever going to jog her memory, but her few friends here had stopped asking most questions a while back. A new person meant more questions, and each question caused her to evade and face the blank wall all over again.

"I wasn't trying to pry," he said, lifting his hand for the waitress. When she came over, he asked her to put both coffees in takeout cups, and the blueberry muffin remains in a bag.

Afterward, he passed the bag to Julie. "Sorry I cut it into mostly crumbs. I thought we had a little longer. It's been great getting to know you. Thanks for the company, Julie."

"Thank you for the coffee and muffin." She stood and

pulled her coat on quickly, not so quickly that she appeared to be in headlong flight, she hoped.

He stood, too, offering to shake her hand. She took it reluctantly, and once again met those brown eyes. They seemed to hold some kind of understanding, although what he was understanding she couldn't imagine. She was acting like a nut.

"See you soon," he said, and let her make her way out on her own. He watched her get into her car and drive off, and it wasn't until she was out of town and nearing her cabin that she realized just how tense she had become; that reaction was making her shake.

One man, one coffee, a few casual questions and she became a basket case? God, she had to get over this. He appeared interested in her. She knew for a fact that she was interested in him. Then she turned into a nut and ran from what she wanted?

Oh, she definitely had to get over this, at least enough to reach for the future.

But the only way over it seemed to be recovering something that remained stubbornly elusive: her past.

Chapter Three

Braden wasted a lot of time over the next couple of weeks wondering about Julie and what her problem was. Since he spent the time doing manual labor around the family spread, the mindless kinds of tasks he needed to do for the most part opened up his mind to wander—and no matter what he did to distract himself, it kept wandering right over to the mysterious blonde.

Pitching hay and stacking bales didn't exactly require many brain cells. Making sure it would be easy to feed the cattle when the snow got deep, making sure the bales provided windbreaks against the worst weather, took a lot of time but not a lot of thought.

So he was thinking about Julie and telling himself he was a fool. At least Dallas was over on a different section of their pastures, because he would have noticed his woolgathering and given him a hard time about it. Someplace deep inside, he did *not* want to be teased about his fascination with Julie Smith.

That alone should probably have warned him, he thought almost grimly.

What was it about the woman anyway? She seemed frightened of almost everything, poised on the edge of taking flight…and then she'd relax briefly, and he was sure he saw the real woman peek through. Maybe.

Will the real Julie Smith stand up? he thought with

sour amusement. She looked so innocent, so angelic with those big blue eyes, that he couldn't believe there was anything bad about her. She'd been in town since June, and there sure hadn't been any unkind whispers about her. If she were a bad sort, he'd have heard something by now.

But even on the rumor mill it was almost as if she were invisible, which was kind of hard to do. People who knew her mentioned her briefly; she did things with the Newcomers Club; she'd made some good friends. Upstanding friends. If they thought there was anything wrong with her, they wouldn't keep her in their circle.

So whatever was going on had to be something other than that she was a fleeing felon.

He almost laughed at that thought. Yeah, right.

But the urge to protect her remained; the desire to know more about her goaded him. The coffee experience…well, he didn't know for sure how to characterize that. Maybe she *had* just had something to do. After all, the meetup had been impromptu, and she could well have had some chores awaiting her.

He slung another bale onto the wall he was building to give the cattle a windbreak, and hoped like hell that Winona Cobbs was wrong about a record-breaking blizzard on its way. The weather reports certainly showed no indication of any big front coming, even as far away as the Pacific Coast. So far it looked as if they were in for a relatively normal December.

He didn't want to ponder Winona, however. She could be intriguing at times, but mostly he thought of her as a character, part of the charm of the place. For some reason, that brought his thoughts around to another character, Homer Gilmore. The old coot was a little crazy, wandering around and telling everyone he was "The Ghost of Christmas Past."

Weird, but the weather was going to take a severe turn for the worse eventually, and he couldn't imagine that Homer could get by relying on charity handouts. Lord only knew where the guy was sleeping. Grunting as he hefted another bale, Braden decided that something needed to be done for the man. Surely there was a warm hidey-hole somewhere in this town where they could shelter him for the winter. If it came to it, Braden would pay for it himself.

It would be heartless to leave the man's fate to the elements.

His mother's remark floated back to him, and he suddenly grinned. Parsival, huh? If she had any idea where his thoughts wandered on the subject of Julie Smith, she wouldn't liken him to a "pure and perfect knight." Hah!

A laugh escaped him even as Julie rose in his mind's eye. That wool sheath she had worn to the pageant had draped her gentle curves in a way that drew a man's thoughts far from the angelic. Her face might bring to mind an angel, but the rest of her called to a man's demons.

He paused for some coffee from his thermos and wiped his brow. Cold or not, a man could work up a sweat doing this. And apart from sweat, there was the damn prickly hay. It had managed to get inside his jacket, and probably his shirt.

He scratched a bit, letting his mind wander over Julie's gentle curves. Closing his eyes as he sipped warming coffee, he imagined running his hands over them. Even through that wool sheath they'd be able to set him on fire. Hell, picturing them was enough to put his motor in high gear.

Leaning back against the wall of hay, he gave himself up to the daydream for a few minutes. Julie in his arms. Her lips welcoming his kiss, her soft curves pressed against his hardness. He imagined pulling down the zipper on that dress, reaching inside to feel warm, silky skin.

Damn it! His eyes popped open, and he stopped himself in midfantasy. Just that little bit, and he was ready to bust out of his jeans. Over a woman he hardly knew, one who seemed a damn sight too skittish to be interested in any kind of intimacy. In fact, she seemed to be avoiding it.

Mentally, he stomped down on his male urges as if he was trying to put out a small grass fire. *Cool it*, he ordered himself.

It might have been easier to call a halt if he hadn't remembered that tomorrow was the Presents for Patriots event at the Community Church. Holy hell. He was going to see her again, and it suddenly struck him that she might spend the whole time avoiding him.

He drained his coffee, wondering if he should skip the whole evening, then realizing he'd never hear the end of it if he let down the Traub family by failing to appear.

Stuck, he thought. Shaking out his cup, he then screwed it back onto the thermos and hit those bales again with every bit of energy in him.

Work could drive out demons, even if it couldn't make him forget an angelic face.

Living a lie didn't make Julie happy. And while she was mostly engaged in just surviving while she hunted for some evidence of her past, it didn't make her happy to realize that she was surrounded by a web of deceit of her own making.

Vanessa and Mallory called a couple of times, asking

what she was up to, and the lie came too easily to her lips. "Writing," she said.

Because that was her cover story. She had to explain why she was hanging out here, why she didn't have a job—mainly because she wasn't at all sure she could hold much of a job successfully. She'd managed working in retail shops and one antiques store, but the strain had overwhelmed her. All the strangers, her uncertainty about so many basic things, the other employees who asked way too many questions about her…well, she had a little money now, thanks to selling that coin, and that meant she didn't have to try to pull off the role of a shopgirl while she was here, a huge relief for her. In a town this size, her seeming standoffishness would eventually be noted and commented on.

So she claimed to be working on a novel on the cheap laptop that sat on a wooden table. It explained how she survived, why she didn't have an ordinary job and why she disappeared sometimes when she felt too troubled.

But it was a lie. She hated the lies so much that she'd even taken a stab at writing something. The problem was, fiction seemed like a way to escape the really important things she needed to deal with, and nonfiction all came down to "My journey as a woman without a memory." As if.

It didn't help that her life seemed like a plot ripped out of the pages of a novel, or that her writing was mostly a meandering diary.

So she wasn't being honest with her new friends, which didn't make her feel one whit more comfortable. Maybe she should just blurt the truth, tell everyone that she'd been born and given a name only a short time ago. Yeah, they'd probably call her crazy and drop her like a hot potato. Who was going to believe that?

So much had happened in the weeks after she returned to awareness of where she was, things that had made her feel that even professionals suspected she might be lying, and finally just made her feel like a bug under a microscope.

Go forth and build a life sounded easy, but it was hard.

Like coffee with Braden. It should have been so simple, but the evasions began to get to her. You couldn't have a relationship based on lies, and the truth was too painful.

Pulling on her outdoor gear, she decided to take a walk in the woods. She left her phone behind, even though she knew she should take it in case she had an accident, but she didn't want another call reminding her about tomorrow, asking how her writing was going, and did she ever intend to come out of her cave.

For the first time she wondered how anyone wrote a book when people were so disrespectful of a writer's time. But maybe writers learned not to answer the phone, not to go to the door, not to feel guilty for ignoring a friend's call.

Somehow she doubted it. Her acquaintance with guilt was growing by leaps and bounds. She seemed to be building it constantly and adding to it with every evasion.

Telling herself it was necessary didn't much help.

They'd tried to convince her that she would be building a new past for herself each day that went by. It sure wasn't enough of a past to satisfy her. Yes, she could talk lightly about the few jobs she'd held in her wanderings, some of the people she'd met, but there was always that wall she couldn't surmount.

Dang, she thought, scuffing her toe in the light layer of snow and bringing up some loam from beneath.

Braden. He was another problem. Though she didn't

have a lot of experience she remembered so she could call on it, she was almost certain that he'd looked at her several times with male interest.

Well, she'd looked at him the same way. He drew her, attracted her, made her want to be a normal girl who could just date and get to know a guy. But since there wasn't much he could get to know about her, she was a fool to even cherish such dreams, and even more of a fool when he hadn't tried to reach her in over a week.

But she couldn't help wishing, and Braden made her wish. The warm, roughness of his palm when he shook her hand seemed to have imprinted itself vividly on her memory. She liked just looking at him, which she supposed was utterly silly, and she reacted like a woman to his scent, to his broad shoulders, to the sight of his butt in those snug jeans he wore.

Oh, man, the bug had bit, but it couldn't go anywhere. Not unless she told him the truth, and she could just imagine the horror that would come to his face. "You don't know who you *are*?" The question that most terrified her.

For heaven's sake, she didn't even know how old she was. When her birthday was. Who her parents had been. Where she had gone to school. All those simple but important things. Not even whether she was a virgin.

Man. Self-disgust filled her again, even though she knew it wasn't fair. She'd been seriously injured. She was lucky to be alive.

Except that she had only part of a life.

Tomorrow was going to be another rough day unless she found a way to excuse herself from the big community gift wrapping. But no, she wasn't going to excuse herself. She had no idea what had drawn her to this town, what had made her feel so compelled to come here, and hiding out wasn't going to answer the question.

But that compulsion… As she stepped out of the trees and looked up, she saw the snowy peaks of the Rocky Mountains, like the Alps, although how she knew that, she had no idea. They called to her, those mountains in all their majestic height and cragginess. They seemed to be a part of her.

They felt more like home than anything else since her accident. They kept her here.

The church hall was full of people by the time Julie arrived. So many people, all very busy at sorting through gifts and wrapping them, then labeling them for "A soldier" or "A soldier's family." Ages were placed only on toys.

Vanessa grabbed her at once and dragged her to the table where she, Mallory and Lily were busy wrapping things.

"The others will be here later," Vanessa told her. "Except Jonah, who has a bad cold. Caleb's finishing some work, and Cecelia and Nick got delayed. I don't want to know how they got delayed." Vanessa rolled her eyes suggestively, drawing a laugh from Julie, who then greeted everyone and asked, "If we were going to do toys, why not send them to Toys for Tots?"

"We work with what people give us," Mallory explained. "Sometimes I think we send enough cologne and aftershave to perfume the entire military."

Julie laughed and allowed herself to relax. This wasn't going to be so hard. "So it really gets to the troops? I thought the military was difficult about that, and these are wrapped." Where that came from, she had no idea.

"It's all going to nearby bases. No problem there. They know who we are."

"Ah."

Lily spoke. "I can't get the triangle right."

At once Julie leaned over to her and showed her how to fold the paper at the end of the package. Sometimes it amazed her that she could remember to do things like this without remembering she had ever done them before.

"I like the triangles," Lily said. "They're prettier than just sticking lots of tape on."

"You're right about that," Julie agreed.

Lily triumphantly placed the last piece of tape and looked up with sparkling eyes. Then she looked past Julie. "Hi, Braden. Are you and Julie friends now?"

"We're working on it," came the answer.

Julie was almost afraid to turn around, but after taking a breath she did, and found him smiling at her.

"Room at this table?" he asked.

"Of course," said Vanessa, scooting over before Julie could respond, making room for him right beside Julie.

It seemed more than Lily were involved in a little matchmaking, Julie thought. Her cheeks heated.

"Hi," he said, still smiling.

"Hi," she managed to answer, then quickly dragged her gaze back to the half-wrapped package in front of her. He looked good enough to eat, and her heart speeded up nervously. He smelled good, too, fresh from a shower, not wearing any aftershave or cologne that she could detect. For some reason she had never found that attractive in a man. At least not in her present incarnation.

He chatted pleasantly with the others who joined the table, appearing comfortable with everyone. She envied him that comfort. Sometimes she wondered if she had ever been someone who had a circle of family and friends that she had known for a long time, a group of people where any reasonable conversation was easy. Small talk certainly didn't come easily to her now, not at all.

And less so, being crowded against him at the table. Inevitably their arms and shoulders brushed, and sometimes they reached out simultaneously for the tape. Each contact, however minor, seemed to zap her with electricity.

A different kind of electricity than she had felt from Winona Cobbs. This kind made her start wondering what it would be like to have this man's arms around her, his lips on hers.

She tried to imagine it and wondered if her imaginings had any basis in experience, or if she was just making it up. How would she know? The not knowing was apt to drive her crazy. She ought to be getting used to this discombobulation, but it didn't seem to be getting any easier, not with a handsome, sexy man standing so close.

"Julie? Julie?" Vanessa's voice punctured her preoccupation. She snapped her head up.

"I'm sorry. Woolgathering."

"Nothing new in that," Vanessa teased. "The tape, please?"

Julie leaned over and passed her the dispenser. Somehow that twist and lean brought her hard up against Braden's side.

In an instant, everything else vanished. A web of desire cast its spell, making all her worries and wondering seem like a waste of time. All that mattered was that man and what his closeness was doing to her. What she'd like him to do with her.

Mallory excused herself to take Lily to the bathroom. Vanessa went off in search of a cup of coffee. All of a sudden she was alone with Braden, who was busy cutting paper for the next package.

Desperate not to appear like a dummy, and certainly not disinterested when he was filling her thoughts so much, she hunted for something to say. "Does everyone in town help with this?"

"Of course not." He flashed her a grin. "Some folks are working, some don't have time, some don't care, and could you imagine trying to fit all of Rust Creek into this place? Nah, we'll stay a short while, and you'll see new faces start to arrive."

"That makes sense. How did *you* find time?"

"I worked extra hard the last few days."

She dared to eye him. "Not with barbed wire, I presume."

He laughed. "Nope. Hay. And you know what? That's almost as bad when it finds its way inside your clothes. Prickly and itchy."

"But no danger of stitches."

He looked up from the package he was wrapping, and their gazes engaged. Julie felt as if the air had vanished from the room.

"No stitches," he agreed. Then, "Julie?"

"Jennifer."

He looked startled, but probably no more than she. Where had that come from? She stared at him without seeing him as her mind once again jumped on the hamster wheel. Jennifer? Somehow that sounded right, better than Julie. My God, was that her real name? But for once, something felt as if it fit.

"Julie?" he repeated. "What's wrong?"

She shook herself out of the moment, promising herself she could ponder this revelation later. "Sorry," she said. "It's just that I used to go by Jennifer. I don't know how it came about, it just did. I haven't used it here." Because she didn't know it. "I shouldn't have blurted that."

"Well, if it's the name you prefer, I don't mind using it." His smile was friendly as he returned to wrapping. "Jennifer it is. I like it. Or can I call you Jenn? I like that, too."

Only then did it strike her how many people were going to wonder about this name change. How many questions she might have to answer. Oh, God, she needed to stop blurting things like that. Not that there were too many of them so far.

"Oh, just stick with Julie," she dared to say. "If I go changing my name now, everyone's going to get confused."

"I doubt it. It's your nickname. I think most of your friends would like knowing that."

"I don't know. It seems stupid after all this time to come out with that."

"Let me handle it."

She was glad to, but wondered why he should even bother. Or why she should let him. God, she'd like to find some backbone and take control of this roller-coaster ride she lived on.

Then she reminded herself that she'd had the gumption to move clear across the country on her search to make a new place for herself in an entirely strange town. That wasn't cowardly. She only grew skittish when dealing with people who came close, close enough to figure out that something was wrong with her.

Maybe she should stop making such a big deal out of that. Maybe it was high time she let go of all her anxieties, stiffened her shoulders and let the chips fall wherever.

It sounded good. Not so easy to do.

The room was becoming truly crowded with people now, everyone talking and wrapping presents. Exactly the kind of situation that made Julie nervous. She returned greetings pleasantly enough and began to wonder how soon she could gracefully bow out. Wrapping gifts for the troops and their families seemed important, so she forced herself to attend only to the work. Still no Caleb or Nick.

Vanessa returned with coffee in a covered cup, and Mallory and Lily returned only long enough to bid everyone farewell. "Bedtime for the pip-squeak," Mallory said.

"I am not a pip-squeak," Lily insisted. "I don't squeak much."

Mallory squatted. "No, you don't. And it was meant to be affectionate, not a bad name."

Lily frowned. "I don't like the way it sounds." Then she looked at Julie-Jennifer and Braden. "You keep making friends," she said. And an instant later she was skipping toward the coatroom with her aunt in tow.

Vanessa's cell phone rang, and a frown lowered on her face. "Well, I'm outta here, too," she said after she disconnected. "There's a problem at the hotel. See you later."

"Watching that woman work on the hotel design is purely an experience," Braden remarked. "She sees things I'd miss."

"Artistic eye." Or maybe Jonah needed her. Now she was alone at the table with him, and her discomfort grew. Surely someone else would join them? But they were almost done with the rack of gifts that had been given to them. Nobody, it seemed, had to do that much. Many hands and all that.

"Say," he said as he reached for the last gift, this one a set of scented soaps. "Why don't we try the coffee thing again, Jenn? I hate to head home without my latte."

Considering how she'd fled the last time, she might

have said no. But temptation was standing there in a fantastically gorgeous package, and he had just called her Jenn. Hearing that name on his lips warmed some place inside her that hadn't felt warm in a long time. She couldn't resist, though some wiser part of her cried that she might be making a big mistake. Blowing her cover. Revealing her inadequacies.

"Sure," she heard herself say. "I'd like that." Who was running her mouth now? Julie or Jennifer?

"Good." He wrapped paper around the last package and asked her to hold it with her finger while he reached for the tape. "I was afraid I'd offended you last time."

"Me? No!" The thought horrified her. "No, Braden. I just had…something I needed to do."

He turned his head, and his eyes smiled at her. "I'm glad to know that. I don't usually send people into head-long flight to get away from me."

She felt her cheeks burn. "I'm sorry. I didn't mean to make you feel like that."

"Which you just proved by agreeing to go out with me again. Hey, lady, it's my evening out, my day off. I'd enjoy it a lot more with your company."

A very kind and flattering thing to say, and pleasant heat shot through her. Maybe she was walking on a tightrope, but in this instance, the fall might even be fun.

Twenty minutes later they once again sat in the donut shop. It being Saturday night, it was packed, but they managed to grab one of the few small tables. Once again they both ordered the same things.

"I've been talking to Homer Gilmore," Braden said. "Do you know who he is?"

"I've seen him around, but no one seems to know his story."

"No one does, at least, no one I've talked to," Braden

agreed. "I'm working on getting him a place to stay, maybe at the church, before he freezes to death out there."

Jenn—she really *did* feel better thinking of herself that way, perhaps another piece of the mystery solved?—shook her head. "He seems sad. I hear he doesn't even say anything intelligible."

"That's part of the problem. He wanders around mumbling unintelligible stuff, and nobody knows what to make of him. He seems harmless. I mean, he's been hanging around and hasn't really bothered anybody, unless mumbling crazy things to people is bothersome."

Jenn felt herself warm to him even more. "It's kind of you to try to find a place for him to stay."

"Not really. He deserves at least as much care as any stray, don't you think?"

Considering she was a stray of sorts herself, she nodded. "Don't diminish what you're doing. I don't see anyone else running around trying to find the guy a home."

He leaned back as they were served and gave her a crooked smile. "If Winona's right, I need to get cracking."

"She's still predicting that blizzard?"

"Not only that, but every time she gives a prediction, it seems to have grown bigger and worse. Which brings me to a question. Are you going to be okay in that cabin if the power goes out?"

"I was thinking of getting a kerosene heater."

He shook his head. "Better to use the woodstove. If you want, I'll check it out for you when we leave here, make sure the chimney is clean."

"That thing looks like a monster to me."

He laughed quietly. "It's not. I'll make sure it's safe then show you how to light a fire. Have you got any wood out there?"

"Some, alongside the cabin."

"I guess you couldn't tell me how much."

Surprisingly, she felt herself smile then laugh. "What I know about wood you can put on the head of a pin. There's a stack. I have no idea how much or how long it would last."

"A very good reason to take advantage of a willing neighbor. Me."

Take advantage of him? She hoped he had absolutely no idea the visions that wording brought to her head. "Well," she said, "if you're going to do that for me, I ought to stop by the grocery before it closes and pick up what I need to feed you a late meal. Unless you've already eaten."

"I haven't but it's not necessary," he said. "Which is not to say I wouldn't enjoy it. I just don't want you to feel obligated."

She was almost relieved by his refusal, but then relief gave way to disappointment. She really *did* want to spend time with this man, even though it would mean tiptoeing through the minefield of evasions and nonanswers.

Torn again. She was getting tired of *herself*, she realized. "It'll be something simple, and I'd really like to do it, if you have time."

"I have time. Okay, that would be great. But when we're done here, I need to stop by the church again. I've been working on the rev to turn over some storage space to Homer. It's empty now." His eyes sparkled. "All those gifts will be shipped on Monday, and there's this nice warm room."

She laughed again. "I think you're going to win."

"It's not winning. He's a charitable man. It's just that no one is really comfortable with Homer. I think the good reverend is afraid he might burn the place down or something."

Jennifer nodded. "That's not an unreasonable fear."

"The thing is, while I think Homer may be crazy, I don't think he's stupid. There's a huge difference. He's made it this far under worse circumstances. I'd find him space at our ranch, but he wanders too much, and he'd be even more alone. No, he needs to be in town where someone can make sure he's okay and that he's eating."

"Do you often collect strays?" The question wasn't as light as she tried to make it sound. She hoped she wasn't another stray like Homer to him.

"Me? Nah. Now when I was young, yes, but now?" He shook his head. "If I find them, I put them at the shelter for adoption. Sometimes I don't find them in time." His face darkened.

"What do you mean?" That look on his face made her nervous. She liked it better when he looked happy. Plus, she wondered if he had deliberately diverted the subject from stray people to stray animals. She desperately hoped he didn't see her that way.

"Just that people dump pets they don't want on the ranches and farms. I guess they think the animals can take care of themselves. Well, they can't. They don't know how. So unless we find them…" He shook his head. "Sorry, that's a downer. How about a more cheerful topic?"

"Got one?" she asked, again trying to sound light.

"Of course. I'm a generally cheerful guy."

But before either of them could say another word, a familiar voice interrupted.

"Well, well," said Dallas Traub. "Look who's having coffee with the new lady."

Jenn wanted to sink into the floor. Braden looked annoyed, and his evident annoyance appeared to grow as

Dallas grabbed a chair and turned it around so he could sit at the end of their booth.

"Dallas, cut it out. Jenn's not used to us."

"Jenn?" Both of Dallas's brows elevated. Julie-Jenn—which was it?—wished him to the devil as her crazy name change came out in the worst way possible.

Braden didn't give her a chance to speak. "We just came from wrapping presents. Did you do yours?"

"On my way there as soon as I get coffee for me and Nina, and hot chocolates for the kids. So what's with the name?" Clearly he wasn't going to let it drop. Just then, one of his young sons, dressed in a puffy down coat, came bursting through the door and ran up to him. He tugged the bottom of Dallas's jacket, and the man reached out and arm to hold him close. Braden gave the boy's shoulder a squeeze, though he was busy staring at Dallas.

"Simple," said Braden in a voice that seemed edged with warning steel. "It's her nickname. She shared it with me while we were wrapping presents. Seems only courteous to call a lady by the name she prefers, without making a big deal about it."

Dallas lifted both hands, palms out. "Easy, brother, easy. I was just curious." He smiled at Julie. "Hi, Jenn. That is, unless only my bachelor brother is allowed to use the name."

"God, Dallas." Braden nearly groaned.

"I don't mind anyone using it," Jenn answered bravely. "After all these months, though, I'll probably need to get used to it again. Who's your adorable shadow here?"

Dallas chuckled. "This is my youngest, Robbie." The boy gave Jenn a shy smile but stayed close to his father. "As I was saying, there's names and there's names.

You know, like Mule here. That's what we used to call Braden."

"Until I got big enough to shut some mouths," Braden said.

"He's still stubborn," Dallas went on as if his brother hadn't spoken. "Makes up his mind, and that's it. Or in the case of women, never makes up his mind." He looked at Braden. "So tell me, man, are you waiting for some kind of perfect female saint? It'll take one to put up with you."

At that moment, the waitress put a cardboard tray full of cups in front of Dallas.

"Daddy, hurry," said the boy.

"That's your cue," Braden said firmly.

Dallas laughed. "I can take a lead-footed hint." He looked at Julie. "Jenn. I like it. Good nickname. But look out for this guy. Love 'em and leave 'em, that's him."

"Damn it, Dallas!"

Still laughing, Dallas stood up and put the chair back. Grabbing his coffee, he headed for the door. Alongside him trotted his son, who was asking in a piping voice, "You really called Uncle Braden a mule?"

Jenn sat waiting quietly, not quite sure what to say.

"Numbskull," Braden said. "That should be *his* nickname. And he's wrong. But you try getting to know a woman with those guys always butting in like that. Are you ready to shake me off? I wouldn't blame you because I come with all of that attached."

Jenn hesitated. She was beginning to feel scattered inside, between her new name and the things Dallas had said and Braden talking as if they already had some kind of relationship. A bit uncertain how to proceed. God, she wished she knew who she was. "We're just having coffee," she said finally. "No biggie. Right?"

The warmth in his brown eyes seemed to deepen. "No biggie," he agreed. "Just friends having coffee."

"Then I'm not shaking you off. Even because of Dallas."

He smiled then. "You're braver than most, Ju-Jenn."

Somehow that struck her as funny. She giggled. "You poor man."

"Most of the time I don't mind it," he admitted. "Except when they get ham-fisted at the wrong time."

"Which apparently happens sometimes."

He nodded. "As just proved."

She relaxed then, somehow feeling comfortable with him. He'd been the one most disturbed by Dallas; he hadn't done one thing to make her feel uneasy, and he'd handled the name business beautifully. She was content to sit and listen as he talked casually about the kind of winter preparations they were making at the Triple-T, and the things they'd be dealing with in the months ahead. He was clearly a very busy man.

Before long, they were done with their coffee. As they rose, he said, "I'll meet you at your place. Maybe half an hour or a little longer, depending on how much time I spend at the church. We'll master that monster stove."

Damn, he was charming, she thought as he walked her to her car and opened the door for her. She waved to him as she backed out.

Then the dam broke. Who was Jennifer? Was she really Jennifer? She turned the name around and around in her head, feeling it, tasting it, finding it seemed to fit comfortably on her, like a warm shawl on a chilly day. Okay, so she was Jennifer. Whoever Jennifer was. She wondered how her friends would react to this news, because she suspected it would get around even if she didn't say anything herself.

But why *shouldn't* she say anything? If she felt more comfortable with that name, she could explain it the same way she had explained it to Braden. He'd accepted it easily enough.

Somehow, she promised herself for the millionth time, this was all going to be okay. She'd make it.

Chapter Four

She stopped at the market just in time and got the ne-
cessities to make Chicken Cordon Bleu, actually a very
easy recipe despite the fancy name. It would be nice if
she could remember how she had learned to make it. Or
all the times she must have made it in the past.

On the way back to her cabin, tension began to creep
into her again. Dallas had acted as if it were a big deal
that Braden was having coffee with her. What did that
mean? Just brotherly teasing? Or something more?

She'd already heard more than once that Braden was
the last single Traub, but she couldn't understand why
that seemed like something worthy of mention. He wasn't
all that old. Were people supposed to get married out of
the cradle here?

But even with her lack of memory, she sensed that
Braden's interest in her was more than casual. That could
become a problem. She knew it but didn't want to call a
halt. Not yet. Twice now she'd been with him when she'd
had a flash of her past. Maybe he had nothing to do with
it, but what if he did?

Then she forced herself to shrug the thought aside. An
attractive man was showing interest. That was a good
thing, even if it didn't last long. She needed that kind of
reassurance, although again she didn't know why. Maybe

because she'd been feeling so unsure of herself and everything else?

Regardless, she was attracted to him, and despite her nerves was looking forward to having him over, to his help with the stove, and to sharing dinner with him. It shouldn't cause much talk because she was definitely off the beaten track out here. Nobody would probably even find out, which might keep his brothers off his back, and her friends from teasing her, as well.

She ought to be able to take the teasing, but the truth was, she was so aware of what she lacked that she sometimes felt fragile and unsure about how to respond. Which made her a weakling, she supposed, and she had no reason to feel weak.

Stiffening herself, she carried the groceries inside and began to get ready for dinner. She was a woman who had chased her own identity all over the country. She was tough. She could handle just about anything.

Finally smiling, she began to hum. Enough of herself. Time to think about having a man over for a little while. Because anyway she looked at it, it struck her that they were having a date. Of sorts.

By the time Braden drove up, she had the rolled chicken cutlets in the fridge, awaiting cooking. A pan of flour and paprika stood ready for coating them, the ingredients for the wine sauce waited at hand, and she debated which vegetables to serve with it. Well, she supposed she could ask him what he preferred.

Overall, it was an easy meal to make, but she'd gone a little overboard on her budget by buying ham and Swiss cheese to stuff the breasts, and white wine for the sauce. A little splurge, but surely she deserved one for a special occasion?

And surely Braden deserved a special meal for doing all of this for her. She was still regarding the woodstove dubiously, and wondered if he'd be able to banish her fear of it.

The phone rang. It was Vanessa, proving that in a town this size, gossip flew faster than the speed of light. "I hear," she said knowingly, "that you had coffee with Braden Traub."

"I wouldn't have thought that interesting enough to be worthy of mentioning." A lie. She herself had certainly found it interesting.

"Dallas mentioned it. Apparently, he's gloating that his brother has been snared."

"Because of a cup of coffee?" Jenn blinked in astonishment.

"Oh, he's just being an annoying brother. It's not like Braden hasn't dated before. They just like to give him a hard time, those brothers of his. From what I've seen, he gives as good as he gets. But that's not really why I called. Coffee doesn't add up to wedding bells."

"No, really it doesn't. What's up?"

"Your nickname."

Something inside Jenn or Julie or whoever froze and tried to curl into a tight knot. "Why?"

"Listen," Vanessa said, "I'm not trying to give you a hard time. I just wondered if Dallas was making up stuff or if that really is your nickname."

"It was," Jenn answered as truthfully as she could.

"I wish you'd told us all. I hate to think we've been calling you by a name you don't like. So it's Jenn or Jennifer? Middle name?"

Jenn didn't know how to answer that. Honestly, she was getting confused by this herself.

After a moment, Vanessa spoke cheerfully. "Well, I

like it. So okay, I'll tell the others. Jenn or Jennifer. It'll probably feel more like home around here if we use your nickname."

"Thank you." Jenn felt a wave of warmth toward Vanessa. "How'd the problem at the lodge go?"

"No biggie. Someone dinged my mural and I needed to touch it up. Time is getting so tight, Nate is afraid to let anything wait."

"And Jonah? How's he feeling?"

Vanessa laughed again. "Men, like mighty oaks, fall hard when they get sick. I need to take him some more chicken broth. Talk to you soon?"

Jenn disconnected and leaned back against the counter, waiting for Braden with more impatience than she would have believed possible. And wondering at the same time about this Jennifer thing. It fit, it felt right. It felt like it belonged to her more than the name Julie. But still, how could she be sure? Sure or not, she definitely liked having Braden call her Jenn, so Jenn it would be.

Did it matter? Finally, she shook her head once again, and her fingers wandered up to feel the long scar in her scalp, a scar successfully covered by her hair.

She would never know what had happened to her, and she would never, ever be really sure if any memories she regained were real. Not unless she ran into someone who had known her before.

Oddly, that scared her. Wouldn't confirmation be a positive thing? But it could also turn into a kind of misery, she supposed, a person or people who knew a past that she'd forgotten. It might answer some general questions, but it would give her very little. A name, a few recollections that would seem like they belonged to someone else. Maybe it would be best if it never happened. Yeah, she wanted to know who she had once been, like it or not, but she also feared the discovery. The thought that she might not like her old self plagued her.

Sometimes she thought it would be best to just let it go. To never know, the way she would never know what had happened to leave her with a cracked skull and no memory. She was *sure* she didn't want to remember that.

But she needed a place, physically and in time. She was trying to build that here, because somehow this town felt comfortable to her. Like something she had once known in the distant mists of time. But there were lots of towns like this, so no way could she know if this was the right one.

But she'd made some small strides toward building a life here, and since she found some strange kind of comfort in this mountain town, she might as well stay and see what happened.

Before she could get too locked in the endless spiral of her thoughts, she heard Braden's truck pull up. A minute later came his knock on her door.

He was smiling as she opened it, and she saw that snowflakes were falling lightly from a sky the color of steel. "Are you ready for me?"

"Absolutely." She stepped back to let him in. "Did things go well at the church?"

"Homer should have a place to stay come Monday. Then the problem becomes finding Homer."

She giggled a little at that. "He seems elusive."

A cold draft had blown in with him and lingered after he closed the door. "Hey, Jenn?"

"Yes?"

"You really need to master this stove. Then you wouldn't be so worried about electric and propane that you keep it this cold."

"I like the cold." She knew that with a certainty she felt for little else in her life these days.

"Not all the time." He astonished her by taking her hand. "Cold fingers. Not good. You need some warming up."

Before she could react, except with a thrill that raced to her very center and made her insides clench with delight and longing, he dropped her hand.

"First things first," he said, becoming all business. "Have you got an old piece of cloth I can drape around the stove?"

"Why would you want to do that?" she asked, surprised. Wouldn't it burn?

"Because if I knock ash and soot out of that chimney, it's going to come out any and every nook or cranny on that thing. Believe me, you don't want soot settling all over this place."

She remembered the old curtains she had taken down when she first moved in. Frayed and aging, they had long since passed any useful life. "I have just the thing."

"Good. Sorry I took so long getting here," he said as she went to the cabin's one closet. "I had to borrow a chimney brush from one of my brothers."

"That must have been fun."

"I didn't have to say much," he laughed. "Apparently, everyone has heard that we had coffee together."

"Vanessa called and mentioned it." She turned with the curtains over her arms and he took them. There wasn't a whole lot of room in this place.

"Well, dang," he said with a wink. "I'd better buy the ring this week."

He made her laugh. It was so easy to laugh with him, despite the winding spring of tension inside her, a tension that eased and strengthened almost constantly as she tiptoed her way into her new life.

A thought struck her. She not only felt maimed in some essential way, but she also felt like an imposter in her own life. Quickly she brushed that idea away for future consideration. How could she be an imposter anyway? She was what she was, just like anyone else.

She watched as he swaddled the stove, covering the door opening completely, and around the base of the chimney.

"The nice thing about the soot," he said, "is that anywhere it turns up on this cloth I'll know if I need to do a little sealing. The air should be getting into the firebox only through the vents. I'll show you how to use them." He paused, looking at her. "You resemble a nervous rabbit."

"I'm just not used to this whole idea. Fire is a scary thing."

"By the time I'm done, you won't be scared, and you'll be ready for winter. Believe me, Jenn, even if we don't get Winona's big blizzard, there'll be other times when power is out, or a propane delivery can't get to you. You can even cook on this stove."

Considering she'd sought this place out, sure that these mountains and winter held some answers for her, she felt like an utter neophyte. She was also feeling wimpy.

"Okay," she said. "I'll put on my pioneer hat."

"Good." His eyes crinkled at the corners as he went back to work.

A short time later he was satisfied. "Okay. I'm going to go get my ladder and the chimney brush. This won't take long."

"I really appreciate this," she hastened to say. She meant it, even though it meant she'd now have no excuse to avoid that stove. Why it loomed like such a large threat in her mind, she couldn't imagine. Maybe she was transferring other anxieties to it. That wouldn't surprise her. "But Braden, it's dark out there."

"There's enough light to do this job. Don't worry."

She listened to his footsteps on the roof. Shortly they were followed by the sound of metal scraping on metal. She could imagine him running the chimney brush up and down the inside of the stovepipe. It must be a messy job.

From inside, however, she couldn't tell how messy it might be. The curtains draped all over the stove successfully prevented any soot from escaping. Ten minutes later, the sounds of his footsteps disappeared from the roof, and she could faintly hear the clatter of his booted feet on the ladder he must have brought with him.

Peeking out the window, she watched him collapse the ladder and carry it back to his truck along with the chimney brush. He was right about the light. The snow seemed to magnify the light spilling from her windows.

Once he had them stowed, he tossed work gloves into a metal box on the bed and headed toward the door. She opened it before he even knocked.

"It was pretty clean," he said. "Either the last resident knew how to build a fire, or he cleaned it before he left. I think I knocked down a bird's nest, though." He must have caught something on her face because he smiled. "Not to worry. It's been empty for a long time."

"Wrong time of year for hatchlings," she agreed, wondering why it had even concerned her. For heaven's sake, it was winter out there, and snow was still falling very gently, just a light dusting.

He began to pull the drapes away from the stove, checking for soot. "A few cracks at the base of the pipe," he said when he was done. "I'll patch them. I have some compound in the truck."

"You carry everything, like a handyman," she said with surprise.

"When you work on a ranch as big as I do, you learn to carry everything you might need." Then he flashed her a smile. "I cheated. I knew I'd be working on the stove, so I stopped at the hardware store." He rolled up the drapes. "Do you want these? The stove is pretty sound, but there's a little soot from the stovepipe. You don't have a washer here, do you?"

"I use the laundry in town. And no, I don't need to save those."

"Then I'll cart them to the dump." He dashed out with them then returned with his work gloves and a can full of something.

It occurred to her then that she wasn't even being a good hostess. "Would you like some coffee? I can make it."

"Sounds great."

She left him to his work while she went to the kitchen area and started the coffee. One big room. Two people could trip over each other in here if they weren't careful.

"That needs a couple of hours to set up," he said. "Then we'll get to fire-making."

Startled to realize that he was right behind her, she almost jumped. God, that was ridiculous, considering that six of his paces would carry him across the entire space.

"Do you want to eat soon?" she asked, hoping her start hadn't been visible.

"Whenever you'd like. But you're stuck with me for a while. Let's have coffee before anything else."

"Sorry it's not a latte."

"Hey, I love coffee any way it comes…except weak."

Soon she was able to fill mugs for both of them, and they settled in the two battered armchairs, one of which she'd tossed the blue blanket over. The angel pillows sat on a scarred wooden chest that looked at least as old as the cabin. As the only seasonal color in the room, they almost looked forlorn.

"You really should have a tree," he remarked.

"Is that your next rescue mission?" She tried to sound light. "The thing is, you're talking about me building a fire in that stove. Where the heck would I put a tree that would be safe?"

He glanced around. "Point taken. But maybe a small artificial one that you could put on the table."

She laughed, suddenly amused. "Knight-errant," she said.

"Oh no, you don't. I swear, I hear enough of that from my mother. Have you been talking with her? I just want you to feel at home here, and it looks like you haven't been able to do a lot so far."

How could she possibly tell him that her commitment to staying here kept wavering like rippling water? She wasn't at all sure she was at journey's end, and doing too much to this cabin seemed like a waste of money, and possibly effort. "I'll think about it."

"Fair enough, and I'll shut my trap." He glanced toward the window. "More snow. I'd better bring in some wood for the fire before it gets buried. Is that your woodpile I saw near the back corner?"

"You tell me. Like I said, I'm a total tyro on wood and woodstoves."

"We're about to take care of that." He drained his mug and rose, reaching for his jacket. "Be right back."

Through the window she watched him dig out his gloves once more, and disappear around the end of the cabin. This place had few enough windows—only two large ones at the front—but it was enough for her.

Before very long, he returned with a hefty armload of wood. He placed it beside the stove in a heavy canvas hammock-type thing she had always wondered about. "There's a box of kindling, too. I'll bring some in. And it might be a good time to think about reading the newspaper occasionally."

He bounced out once again and returned with some more wood. "I'll have to get you more wood. You don't have enough out there to get you through much more than a few days. A really bad blizzard could cut you off for up to a week."

"I guess I should lay in supplies then, too."

"Nonperishables. Seriously, you can cook a lot of things on the top of that stove. Just remember, it's apt to be hot, and you can't control the temperature very well."

He was a good teacher as he led her through the intricacies of how to build a fire and control its output with the vents. "You don't want it to blaze, once you get it started, so you pretty much close the vents. Just let a tiny bit of air in. It'll burn hotter and longer and make less soot."

And so on. She wondered how much of this she would even be able to remember, and if she should be taking notes.

Soon he had a pleasant fire going, and she could feel warmth beginning to seep through the cabin. It was certainly more comfortable than the sixty-six degrees she had the thermostat set to.

"We'll run through this again once I get you some more wood."

She hesitated. He was being awfully generous. "I can order a delivery, can't I?"

"Why should you? We have enough split wood out at the ranch to get us through four years without any other heat. We can spare the little you'll need, no problem."

The fire did make the cabin seem cheerier, especially since she could see the flames through the glass door on the stove.

"I wonder who put that stove in?" Braden mused. "It's a good one, and that door even makes it pretty."

"You're not familiar with who lived here before?"

He cocked a brow at her. "People who live out here tend to keep to themselves. It was kind of a surprising place for you to choose."

She hesitated, then used her cover story. "I was mainly thinking about peace and quiet for writing."

"You're a writer?"

"Hope to be."

He half smiled. "There are all kinds of difficult jobs in the world. I'd put that near the top of the list. I'm doing good if I can write a list of chores."

She was pretty sure he was exaggerating, but there was one thing she could say with perfect truth. "I haven't made a whole lot of progress yet."

"Be patient. It'll come. Most things do."

"I guess I'm going to see."

He offered to help her make dinner, but she declined. Cooking was one of the few tasks where she felt reasonable confidence. Once again she thought how odd it was that she seemed to remember how to do so many things without actually *remembering* them. One thing she knew for certain, however: she felt absolutely no familiarity with a woodstove.

He turned out to be a good dinner guest, keeping her company while she cooked, commenting on how delicious everything smelled. When she brought out the plates and flatware, he insisted on setting her little table for two.

When at last they dined, he took one mouthful of the chicken, closed his eyes as he savored it and announced it was the best thing he'd eaten in a very long time.

"We tend to go simple at the ranch, most of the time. So many mouths, so many varied taste preferences. Mom decided a long time ago that we were beans, potatoes and meat men."

She smiled. "Doesn't look like it at the moment."

"It's just easy, like I said. Must have been really interesting for her when we were youngsters. Six brothers, everyone wanting something different. About the only time we all reached agreement was over hamburgers and hot dogs."

She laughed. "Fun times."

"For us. Not so much for her, probably. I guess we survived our pathetic food tastes because we all liked vegetables of any kind. We have a garden every summer and freeze or can any overabundance."

It sounded so… Well, she couldn't think of the proper word for it, but she liked the picture he was painting of his life. A family. Working together. Growing a garden together. Putting up food for the winter.

She was probably romanticizing a whole lot of work, she warned herself. She'd already heard about the way Braden worked nearly every day, so much so that getting away for a brief stint in town was a rarity, at least for now.

"Does your work slow down in the winter?" she asked.

"If we're properly prepared. We have more free time, some of which goes to taking care of things we've had to let slide during the busy times. Do you ride?"

"Horses?" She blinked, once again facing her internal blank wall. Hadn't he asked this before? Why was he asking again. No, that was whether she skied. And she still had no idea how to answer.

But before her silence became obvious, he spoke again. "If we get some decent weather, I should take you out for a gentle ride. I think you'd love it."

"I think so." She thought she might enjoy it but had no way to know. Maybe once she was on the horse's back, her feelings would change.

Their conversation remained light enough and general enough that she was mostly able to relax and just enjoy his company. He seemed to have a knack for bringing up simple matters, and for entertaining with stories about his childhood. He put few demands on her, and she felt her liking for him growing. An easy companion. Easier than even her girlfriends.

He insisted on washing the dishes while she had after-dinner coffee; he raved about her cooking, and all in all made her feel pretty good.

She smiled more than she had in a long time, and laughed more freely. But she was also very aware that the more time she spent with someone, like her girlfriends, the more danger lurked. Covering up had become almost second nature, but it never ceased to fill her with anxiety.

"Have you visited any of the other towns around here?" he asked her as he hung the dish towel over the stove handle to dry.

"Not really. I've been thinking about it. I picked the wrong time of year to feel a yen to get up into the mountains, I guess."

"Not really. We can still take a drive if you like, maybe over to Thunder Canyon to see my brothers Forrest and Clay and their families. If you feel like it. Say Tuesday? I should be all caught up on chores."

At once she felt herself pulled in differing directions. More time with Braden? Possibly tiptoeing around the rabbit hole in which she seemed to live? But the mountains called to her, and if she were to be honest, so did Braden. Before she could catch herself, she said, "I'd love that." Except for the Thunder Canyon part. She didn't want to go visiting, and wondered how she could divert him from that without being rude.

"Great, I'll give you a call." Then he pointed at the woodstove. "I need to get going before tongues start wagging, but let me show you how to keep that fire banked overnight so that in the morning all you have to do is throw on a couple more logs."

So she squatted beside him in front of the stove. The blast of heat that emerged when he opened the door astonished her, and gave her some indication of how gently the stove was radiating the heat. Yes, she could tell the stove was hot this close, but nothing like the blast-furnace effect of opening the door.

The banking part was something she was sure she could manage. He mounded coals together and scooped ash on top of them. "In the morning all you should have to do is stir this a bit and throw a log or two on top."

"Very cool," she said as he latched the stove door closed.

They were still squatting, and she felt him look at her, so she turned. What happened then seemed as inevitable as the flow of the seasons.

"You're beautiful," he murmured, then leaned toward her until their mouths met.

One of those glowing coals from the stove might have touched her lips. A very different kind of fire instantly ignited in her. God, this felt so good!

She dropped to her knees to keep her balance, and he

never broke the kiss. Without thinking, she raised one hand to grip his shoulder and keep him close.

She couldn't remember ever having wanted anything as much as she wanted this man's kiss. It hit her out of nowhere, like a racing train, fresh, unexpected and utterly powerful. She had never seen it coming, despite the attraction she felt, never guessed that a mere kiss could inflame her so fast and so furiously.

Warm. Gentle. Nothing forceful, nothing demanding. Just a gentle caress.

Then it was gone.

"Oh, very nice," he whispered, then jumped to his feet. "I really have to run. See you Tuesday."

Very *nice*. Nice? That's what he thought? As the door closed behind him, she remained kneeling in front of the stove, and all she wanted to do was cry.

Nice. Her whole world felt as if it had just been turned upside down again and he said *Nice*?

Braden was grateful for the chilly night air. The cold bathed him, and he didn't even turn on the heater in his truck. He'd kissed more than a few women in his life, but his response to Julie—Jenn—had left him feeling like he needed to run fast and hard to save himself.

Because, damn it, one kiss and he'd been on fire for her. Perilously close to sweeping her beneath him on that rug and exploring every nook and cranny of her body until she begged for more.

He knew better than that. What he had just experienced was dangerous in so many ways. She was still the mystery woman about whom he knew very little. He still caught her hesitations when she needed to answer a question, still saw a mixture of doubt and uncertainty in those incredible blue eyes.

Sex would only complicate the entire thing for both of them. It might take them places both of them would regret. Hell, he wasn't a kid anymore. He knew that a relationship had to come first; there had to be some understanding, some friendship, some liking. He liked her so far, but he felt they were a long way from friendship and understanding.

Crap. He was driving too fast and eased up on the gas. The flurries earlier had made this lousy road slippery, and the last thing he wanted to do tonight was call to get towed out of a ditch. If his cell would even get a signal out here. There were still dead zones where a phone wouldn't work, although since last year's flood they'd been trying to improve that, too. And if he got on the satellite phone they used for the ranch, he'd be talking to one of the very people he most didn't want to have to explain himself to. Gradually, he began to cool down, and to wonder what it was about that woman that brought out the devil in him. Why he wanted her so badly. Why he was deliberately inserting himself into her life.

Loneliness? He simply shook his head. He didn't have time to be lonely, and had too many friends and family to need someone else. It was one thing to help her deal with her woodstove, and another to start craving her like a starving man.

But one little kiss, just a teeny little kiss, and everything inside him had responded instantly. Kinda scary.

First he had to solve the mystery of Jenn. Learn more about her, about why she sometimes looked lonely in a crowd, why she seemed to back away from the simplest of questions. What was her secret? What was she hiding from?

Those questions *had* to be answered first.

Well, maybe he'd get some answers during their drive

on Tuesday. Mentally he crossed out any thought of going to see his brothers in Thunder Canyon. He wanted to share his biggest infatuation with Jenn, and Jenn alone. He loved running up some of the roads into the mountains, and the winter still hadn't deepened enough to make it risky. Beautiful vistas, majestic peaks, the deep shadows of the evergreen forests. The place seemed magical to him.

It would be interesting to see Jenn's response. If she didn't feel the magic, too, then he'd know for sure she wasn't for him, at least not beyond casual friendship.

So yeah. He felt a little better. Tuesday he'd find out more about her. Like whether he should ever see her again.

Chapter Five

Jenn joined her friends at church on Sunday morning and heard all about Winona Cobbs's increasingly bad predictions. When she glimpsed Winona Cobbs emerging after the service, she panicked. She didn't know what it was about that woman, but she didn't want to be around her.

"Gotta run," she told Vanessa, Callie, Mallory and Cecelia.

"Hey, what about coffee and donuts?" Callie protested. "We said we would head over to Daisy's this morning."

"I can't, really," Jenn said hastily, watching as Winona grew closer. "I'm in the middle of something in my...writing."

"Okay, then," Vanessa said lightly. "I get it, being an artist and all. Go. Be flaky. Your calling gives you permission."

Jenn would have been a whole lot more amused if she hadn't felt the overwhelming need to flee. Briefly, her gaze met Winona's. She felt again that electric shock, but Winona didn't seem to be interested in her at all. The woman turned away to speak to someone else and Jenn fled.

Writing gave her permission to be flaky? Only as she left town behind did Jenn begin to relax, her anxiety about Winona easing, and Vanessa's remark penetrating. She felt a little bubble of laughter in her stomach but it didn't escape.

So now she had an excuse for being weird? Who would have thought? Instant cover. Just say you're some kind of artist. Maybe they were accepting her name change as the same kind of flakiness.

Anxiety drained away as she pondered the words. An excuse, built in. *Thank you, Vanessa.*

But she also wondered what it was about Winona Cobbs that bothered her so much. She was sure she didn't know the woman, and the woman didn't seem to even want to meet her. So why this reaction, followed by such an urgent need to escape?

Maybe she was a little crazy herself, no artistry to excuse it.

But the hard part of having no memory was lacking touchstones for her own reactions. Maybe Winona reminded her of someone she couldn't remember. Maybe it had been a bad experience.

And she might never know.

What did she have to go on anyway? A name that felt like it belonged to her, a fleeting memory of a Christmas pageant, her reaction to Winona, and her love of the mountains around this town.

Not a whole heck of a lot.

Back at home, she followed Braden's directions and put a few more logs on the fire after stirring the coals. They caught quickly, and soon the cabin was warm, and she nearly closed the air intakes.

Treating herself, she turned her small wobbly desk so she could see the red glow from the fire and decided she could get used to this. Maybe even become proficient at it. Stepping outside, she went to her woodpile to bring in a few more logs.

When she looked at it, she quickly guessed Braden was right about her needing some more wood. She might have enough for a few more days at this rate. Each day that she burned the stove, the pile shrank. Of course, she'd noticed that her heat wasn't turning on, and given the cost of propane for the heater and electric to run the blower, it was probably saving her loads of money. As for the rest…well, there was no way to reduce her electric, and the stove still operated on propane. Maybe she should try cooking on the top of the woodstove. Little things, like an egg, or using the metal percolator she'd found at the back of the cupboard instead of the drip coffeemaker.

A sense of adventure overcame her, and she decided coffee was the safest starting point. She could hear if it started to boil over, and smell when the coffee was ready.

She stacked the pot as best as she could remember, if memory it was, and set it on the stove. Then she sat down to her laptop. Browsing the web tempted her, even on her slow dial-up service, but instead she forced herself to write.

After all, that's what she had said she was going to do.

Her random scribblings weren't very impressive, though. Mostly she'd been keeping a kind of diary, as if somewhere within it she might find answers. It gave her thoughts more order than the mental hamster wheel she too often got stuck in. She had no idea if the order was any more useful, but sometimes she felt reassured that she could look back over her meanderings. A written record couldn't be erased by accident, unlike most of her life.

Because a terrifying possibility kept haunting her. What if she woke up one morning and discovered she had lost the last four years as well as everything that came before? What if she once again woke up a blank slate? It had happened once, and there was no reason to think it couldn't happen again.

Such an event was unlikely to be sure, but recording things on her computer made her feel safer somehow, and she always kept everything backed up on a flash drive, tucked safely away, in case the computer crashed.

So she sat at her computer, watching the fire, and little by little recorded her impressions of her day with Braden, how he'd made her feel, how he'd been so helpful. *A tendril of belonging*, she thought as she typed the words. The girls, and now Braden. Little Lily. People who had come to mean a whole lot to her.

Finally, afraid of getting way too sappy over Braden, who had done nothing but kiss her and call the experience nice, she scrolled back through the other things she had written down.

Lifting her hand, she fingered the tarnished coins that hung around her neck. She wore them all the time, but not because she had learned they were worth a lot of money. They were all she had left of her former life, for one thing, but even more important, they might be recognized by someone. Hope on that score had nearly died, but she wasn't ready to abandon it yet.

Finally, she shook herself from reverie, pulled the coffee off the woodstove and found it had turned out perfectly. Pouring herself a mug, she sat sipping her coffee, feeling a rare spell of contentment. She had Tuesday and a drive into the mountains to look forward to. She could hardly wait. She hadn't so far dared to go up there all alone, for fear something might happen.

Something bad had happened in her past, and she no longer thought awful things only happened to other people. In a very real way, she had been stripped of her sense of security.

She still had a long way to go. A very long way.

* * *

Monday night, Braden called Jenn to confirm their drive, saying he'd pick her up at ten the next morning. He liked hearing the pleasure in her voice, and didn't mind the ribbing he got from Dallas when he asked his brother to finish up a few things for him.

"Getting a little serious here, brother?"

Braden rolled his eyes. "A drive in the mountains? You gotta be kidding. Way too early for serious."

"I don't know about that. Sometimes it strikes you fast and hard, like a falling rock. Speaking of which, take it easy on those hairpin turns. I hear there have been some rock slides."

"I seem to remember having driven those roads before."

Dallas laughed. "Yeah. Like the time we got a little too liquored up for our own good in our wild youth. Lucky to be alive."

"Sutter's reflexes had something to do with that luck."

"And you screaming 'rock' like a girl."

Braden couldn't help laughing, but then he noticed Dallas's demeanor change. "What?"

Dallas eyed him gravely. "Be careful, Braden. Nobody seems to know a whole lot about her, and she's a bit... quirky. Nina said she thought she was evasive at times."

"I've noticed. Thanks for your concern, but at the moment I'm more interested in solving the mystery than anything."

Dallas let it go, but Braden knew the warning was a fair one. The things he had begun to feel for Jenn were already surpassing mere curiosity. Danger signs loomed on the road ahead.

He could handle it, he decided. He wasn't by any means in too deep yet, and a casual drive in the mountains wasn't likely to get him in much deeper. He could do that with anyone.

As for the flame of desire she lit in him—well, it wasn't the first time that had happened, and he'd made it out in one piece.

Humming, he went back to work, thinking about which route would be best to follow. Dallas was right about rock slides. It might turn out to be a very short drive, indeed.

Tuesday morning, on his way to pick up Jenn, Braden stopped at the donut shop to have them fill a thermos for him, and added a couple of their sandwiches. No telling when hunger might hit or how long this drive might become. That, he knew, would depend on Jenn and the roads.

He was stepping out of the shop when he ran into Winona Cobbs. He smiled at once, asking lightly, "Storm still coming?"

She frowned at him. "Nobody's listening."

"Maybe because the weather forecast is promising clear blue skies for the next week."

She shook her head. "There are things they don't know. Clouds are growing over this town."

"Winona…"

But she cut him off and smiled suddenly. "Don't believe me, Braden Traub. It doesn't matter. Soon enough you'll know." Then she paused. "I want to talk to that girl you're seeing."

Braden hesitated, unsure of what Winona knew or didn't know. Other than his brothers, he figured no one in town knew he'd seen Jenn for more than coffee. Of course, there was no guaranteeing his brothers hadn't gabbed somewhere. They had an unfortunate tendency to make jokes that sometimes revealed too much.

"That girl," Winona said, her gaze growing vague. "Something about her. I want to see her."

"I'll tell her," he said, although he had no intention of doing so. Jenn had been quite up front about how uneasy Winona made her.

Winona's eyes snapped back into focus, fixing on him. "Ignore me, young Traub, and that girl will not find something she desperately needs."

With that, Winona continued on her way. Braden stared after her, wondering what it was with that woman. While he was inclined to believe most of what she said was mumbo jumbo, every so often he had the weirdest feeling that she could see something invisible to others.

Well, if her damn blizzard materialized, he guessed he'd change his opinion.

There hadn't been any snow since Saturday, not even the light flurries they'd had then. The sky overhead was that incredibly clear, almost painful winter blue; the mountains appeared to gleam as if they wore sparkling white coats, and the breeze seemed to be holding its breath.

Jenn hardly waited for him to park the truck in front of her cabin. Her eagerness pleased him as she appeared in her door, waved, then stepped out and locked up. She was dressed for the weather in a decent parka and snow boots, ready for just about anything except getting stranded in the woods. Which wasn't even a remote possibility. He knew the terrain like the back of his hand, and could keep them safe. He even had a few survival skills tucked up his sleeve. Besides, Dallas—and probably the whole family by now—knew where he was going. If he didn't return or call by nightfall, the search parties would be out.

He did manage to climb out and open the passenger door for her before she reached it.

"This is exciting," she said as she slid in. "I've been wanting to get up into those mountains since I got here, but I haven't wanted to do it alone."

"Not in that old beater of yours, reliable as it may be," he agreed. She was making him smile, and he liked it. Imagine a woman being this pleased about a drive in the mountains. In his experience, most wanted more expensive entertainment, or something more exciting. A drive sounded tame, but apparently, not to Jenn.

"Any particular way you want to head?" he asked as he drove away from her place.

"Just mountains. You know the area. I've just been admiring from afar."

"Not very far in this valley. I'll go southwest then. There are some beautiful vistas that open up so you'll get to see more than a tunnel of forest."

"Great!"

"And by the way, I've decided not to go visit my brothers and their families today. Bad timing for them." He patted the insulated bottle on the bench seat between them. "Coffee, if you want. I also got us a sack lunch, so don't be afraid to tell me if you get hungry."

"Maybe later. I just had breakfast."

They didn't talk much as he took a road outside town that linked up with the drive he had chosen. "We won't be able to go over the passes now," he remarked. "Closed for the winter up here."

"Do we get really closed off here?"

"Well, not completely. We can usually head down to Kalispell and from there get most everywhere else we need to go. But we don't have any major roads passing over the mountains here. It gets a little sticky sometimes."

"Around your butt to get to your elbow?"

He laughed. "That's about it. Occasionally, we might

even be cut off from Kalispell for a couple of days until the plows finish, but that's rare. We have pretty good snow removal for the most part."

At last they began the climb, gentle at times, steeper at others, but always winding. He cracked his window just a bit to let in the fresh smell of the evergreens and the slightly sharp one of the fresh snow.

"Have you thought about that Christmas tree?" he asked.

"It seems silly just for me."

"Not if it makes you smile. If you got a very small, real one, think of the way it would scent the cabin."

He felt, rather than saw, her nod as he negotiated a tight turn. The pavement was still black, although a of bit wet from snowmelt could be seen on either side of the road.

"I'm going to have to turn back by one or so," he remarked. "Sorry it can't be longer."

"How come?"

"See how wet the pavement is? That's snow melting. If the temperature starts to drop, it could turn into black ice. Not good."

"Oh. I guess there's a lot I don't know."

"Surely you ran into this in Massachusetts. You did say that's where you're from?"

Again he noted the slight hesitation. "I didn't get out of town much."

"Ah." He let that lie, though he wondered. Didn't get out of town much? What had her life been like before she arrived here? He didn't know how to ask without seeming intrusive. "No car?"

"Public transportation usually. It's great."

Well, he could believe that. She *was* young, and if

there was a convenient alternative, why get a car? "So did you have a job?"

"Yes." That came quickly enough. "My last one was at an antiques store. I spent an awful lot of time dusting and oiling old pieces. They were fascinating, though, and the owner could tell me about most of them. Maybe not specific history, but how they were used. She had this one pharmacy cabinet that she wouldn't part with. It was huge, full of cubbies and drawers with a big counter and cabinets beneath. It might've been the biggest piece of furniture I'd ever seen, and it looked so useful."

"But if it was that big, where would you put it?"

She laughed. "It wouldn't have fit in most rooms, that's for sure. We also sold a lot of old iceboxes, the kind that look like chests, with doors on the front. People liked to use them for kitchen islands, so we were always on the hunt for more of them."

"Did you help with the hunt?"

"Mostly from catalogs and computers. She spent a lot of time traveling to shows to find special things."

"I find the antiques business, um, strange."

He felt her turn in her seat to look at him. "Why?"

He shrugged one shoulder. "One person's junk, another one's treasure, that's all. I'm sure there are pieces in my parents' house that would qualify, and maybe some in my own."

"You have your own house?"

"Of course, right on the ranch. Built most of it myself. I won't mention the help from my brothers. Just a snug little place. But back to antiques. I have a whole thing about that. I mean, we keep a lot of serviceable pieces at our place. Some of them go back to when the family first came west. I bet some of them would fetch a nice price in an antiques store, and I can't imagine why."

She laughed quietly. "I did wonder about some things."

"How could you not? They can need a lot of work, but because they're old, they're worth more?"

"I can see I'll never sell you an antique."

"Probably not," he admitted, and flashed her a grin. "I'm more interested in usefulness."

The switchbacks were coming closer together now, and he fell silent as he paid close attention to the road. As they climbed in altitude, the possibility of ice in shady places grew. No complaints. He liked the quiet; he loved the beauty of the winter woods; he loved being away from everything, and his companion seemed comfortable for a change.

Before long he had slowed to little more than a crawl. Trees and sharp curves occluded sightlines, and he didn't want to come around a tight bend and hit rocks that could take out the bottom of his truck. Cliffs dotted the landscape to either side, not everywhere of course, but enough of them to make him cautious when they weren't rolling between tall trees.

Just as he was thinking it might be best to find a place to turn around and head back, they came around a tight curve and Jenn gasped.

"I dreamed about that mountain!"

He wondered what she meant, but he didn't take time to ask. The rising alpine peak wasn't very visible from town, but up here it seemed to dominate the whole world, and he knew it could be seen from other mountain towns, as well. He looked around until he found a safe place to pull over on gravel and snow, then parked the truck.

The mountain was now concealed by trees again, but he had an idea.

"You like it?"

"It's gorgeous!"

"That's Fall Mountain, quite a landmark. Let's hike back to where you can see it. It'll only take a few minutes, and that's sure a sight to be admired."

She was climbing out before he could help her. He grabbed the thermos, certain that coffee was going to be necessary before long. It was far colder up here than below, and the wind could whip around those curves like a lash.

By the time he climbed out to follow, she was marching steadily back down the road like a woman with a mission. Quirky much? he wondered with amusement. She was certainly different from most of the women he knew. They didn't generally leap out of a car in a hurry to take a look at a mountain.

Something about her determination gave him pause, however, and he followed slowly, feeling that she might need some space, although he couldn't imagine why.

Finally, he reached her side, and she stood looking up at that dang mountain with wonder. Almost awe. Then she said something that stilled everything inside him.

"I belong here."

Her tone warned him that this was important to her, though he couldn't begin to understand what she was driving at. Damn, he needed to figure this woman out, to understand the mystery that made her do things like this.

She belonged here? He suspected she didn't mean on this road. For some reason, that mountain seemed to mean something to her. Well, it was a helluva landmark.

Or maybe she was just responding to the beauty of the place. A lot of people took one look at these mountains and wanted to find a way to stay.

But something in her face seemed to glow. As if she had discovered a treasure.

Then, slowly, it faded. She became aware of him again,

of her surroundings, as if waking from a dream. "How could I know that mountain?" she asked.

He didn't believe she was asking him, so he didn't even attempt an answer. Finally, when she darted an embarrassed look at him, he decided it was time to act as if nothing at all had happened.

"Beautiful view," he said. "Takes the breath away. Want some coffee?"

Jenn refused his offer. She was too entranced by the mountain, and stared up at it for a while longer, feeling something deep within her mind vibrate a response, like a harmonic frequency. She *knew* that mountain. She was sure of it in the way she had been sure the name Jenn fit her.

So she was in the right place. At least, in the right vicinity. If she could have hugged that peak, she might have. It seemed to reach out to her like a call home. Like a mother.

But while she could have stood there forever, even she couldn't ignore the cold indefinitely. It had begun to penetrate her jeans, her parka, and make her ears burn.

A gentle touch on her elbow forced her back.

"We need to go," Braden said. "Sorry. I'll bring you back another time, but right now you're starting to turn blue. Pull up that hood before your ears get frostbite."

Reluctantly, she obeyed, surprisingly glad that the snorkel hood not only warmed her ears but also hid her face a bit. Man, he must think she was nuts.

If he did, though, he gave no sign of it. Once they were back in the truck, he turned them around and headed back down. When he suggested she pour them some coffee, she did so without argument, realizing for the first time how deeply the cold had penetrated.

"Next time we do this," she tried to say lightly, "maybe I should wear some snow pants."

Almost as soon as she spoke, she realized she had inadvertently suggested a second date. She darted a nervous look his way, wondering if his offer to bring her up here another time had been merely polite.

Though he was still driving, he reached sideways and stroked her cheek lightly with the back of his fingers. A hunger for more mushroomed in her instantly. "We're certainly going to make sure you're warmer," he agreed. "Either that or the weather. We might still get a few warm days this month, though. It's only December. Next one we'll come back."

Relaxing finally, she leaned back and sipped the hot coffee. Then he lowered his hand and let it come to rest lightly on her thigh. The heat of his touch penetrated to her very core. Life could feel so good sometimes.

Chapter Six

Three days later, utterly without warning, Winona's predicted blizzard blew in. Nothing on the weather reports had prepared the town, but here it was, blowing like the very devil, the snow falling so heavily it nearly blinded. Icy, too, stinging exposed skin like needles.

Aw hell, Braden thought. The ranch had been prepared; there wasn't a whole hell of lot more he could do in this, but he'd screwed up.

He'd failed to get more wood to Jenn. Thinking he'd had time, remembering her reluctance to use the stove, it hadn't exactly seemed urgent.

After a quick breakfast he hit the woodshed and filled the back of his truck with enough wood for a week or so. Then he went inside the main house for a quick coffee and found his mother and father in the kitchen.

"Everyone's safely in their homes," Bob Traub announced. "Predictions are we'll lose all power, and all of a sudden the weather reports are talking about forty or fifty inches of snow."

"The meteorologists who didn't know anything about this storm?"

"The same. Some kind of anomaly. You can listen to them blather on about how the mountains make their own weather if you want."

"I'll skip it. I promised Jenn I'd bring her a truckload

of wood, and the way it's building out there, I'm not sure I'll be able to see where I'm going before long."

Ellie rose. "Grab food out of the pantry while you're at it. I'm sure that child isn't at all prepared for this."

She probably wasn't, Braden thought. Probably not at all. Twenty minutes later, his father had helped him load a whole bunch of canned goods into the cab along with a three-pound can of coffee. "Must have the essentials," the senior Traub said, winking.

"I don't know if I'll be able to get back."

His father grew serious. "Son, just take care of her. She's a babe in the woods, and this is building from bad to dangerous. And dang me if I ever fail to listen to Winona again."

"She forgot to predict the exact day and hour," Braden retorted. His dad's laugh followed him as he climbed into his truck to go to Jenn.

It was bad, really bad. Whiteout conditions hit from time to time, and it was a damn good thing he could have driven these roads blindfolded. He might as well have been.

Another hour or so, and no one would be going anywhere.

Jenn had heard the wind during the night. It had made the cabin creak a bit, but it was a pleasant sound and didn't frighten her. Besides, she had other thoughts to occupy her, like her reaction to that mountain.

She belonged here? Had she really said that? Really felt it? But when she closed her eyes and cast herself back into that moment, she experienced it all over again. Finally, at long last, she had felt familiarity for something besides a Christmas pageant and a name. Familiarity for a place.

God, she'd been looking for that so long!

She made coffee with the drip coffeemaker. She'd let the fire in the woodstove go out because she was down to her last few logs, and the man she'd called for delivery said he couldn't get to her for a week. She might need those logs, she thought, especially since this previously cozy cabin seemed to have developed a whole bunch of chinks overnight. No matter where she stood, she could feel a strong draft when the wind howled.

Finally, afraid of what she would see, she pulled the curtain back and gasped. She knew a blizzard when she saw one, and this one looked positively evil. How long would it last?

She had no TV because reception here stank. Her computer was hooked into a phone line, so slow on dial-up that she rarely used it for going on the web. Talk about going back to pioneer days. The thought made her almost giggle until she realized that she might be in trouble.

She had taken Braden's advice to stock up on some canned goods, but if the power went out, keeping warm was going to be a problem. The only heat she could make, now that her wood was almost gone, was with her gas stove.

She stood at the window, gnawing at her lip, wondering if she should try to make it to town. What she saw didn't hearten her. The trees surrounding her house almost vanished in the blowing snow. She doubted she'd be able to see more than a foot beyond the front bumper of her car, and she knew she couldn't drive that miserable road blind.

What had possessed her to take this place anyway? In June it had seemed perfect. Right now it felt like madness. She could freeze to death out here.

Just as she was considering the possibility that there

might be more wrong with her than amnesia, she saw Braden's blue truck emerge from the snow like a ghost.

Her heart leaped. He was riding to the rescue. Maybe he'd take her out of here. Although with the conditions so bad…

He pulled up right in front of her stoop and jumped out, bending against the wind as he approached her door, holding his hat on his head. He almost looked like a ghost, too, and in those few steps he actually vanished in the snow twice.

As soon as she heard him pound his feet on the stoop, she opened the door. He darted inside and closed it quickly behind him.

"Do you like living in an icebox?" he asked without even greeting her.

"This place seems to have become leaky overnight. The heater is blasting and it can't seem to keep up."

"I'm not surprised." He pushed his cowboy hat back a little on his head. "I brought wood. I brought food. And you may be stuck with me until this passes. I could hardly see where I was going."

"I was thinking about that just before you appeared," she admitted. "I was wondering if I could get to town, but everything out there is almost invisible." Stuck with him? Part of her wanted to leap exuberantly at the thought. Still…no, she wouldn't even think about her fears over intimacy. If she had to get "stuck" with someone, she was elated that it was Braden.

"We'd have found your frozen body inside your car at the first thaw." He shook his head. "Wise decision to stay here. Let me bring in some wood, and we'll deal with the heat first. Do I smell coffee?"

She had to smile. "Want some?"

"First let me get a few armloads of wood in here.

Dang, you have a lousy heater. Cold as it is outside, I didn't feel a whole lot warmer when I came in."

She couldn't disagree. Dressed in her warmest fleece pants, a heavy shirt and sweater, she still hovered near the point of shivering. "Thanks for coming, Braden," she said sincerely. Just the sight of him made her feel better and less alone. And the thought of having him here through the storm was as pleasurable as it was reassuring. All kinds of sensual possibilities began dancing through her head, an anticipatory excitement she didn't want to shut down. At least not yet.

"Can't leave a pretty lady to become a winter statistic," he said cheerfully, then headed back outside to start unloading the back of his truck.

"Can I help?" she called after him.

"Stay in here where it's warmer. Slightly. A little bit. I'm used to hauling stuff around. Pack mule, that's me."

"I thought it was just Mule."

He laughed as he disappeared into the swirling snow.

A pretty lady? Those words brought a secret smile to her heart and thrilled her deeply. He thought she was pretty. She sure hoped he meant it.

He'd covered the wood on his truck bed with a tarp, so as he brought in four armloads, there wasn't much snow on it to melt.

"I'll get the food in a bit," he said, "and wood as we need it. Let me get this going, then we'll turn off your heat. I think you'll find this blaze will more than make up for it."

She brought him coffee. He drained half the mug in one draft before he started working on the fire. He was amazing to watch, she thought. Every movement sure and practiced. Almost like magic, he soon had flames leaping inside the box. When he at last closed the door, he left the air intakes wide open.

"First we warm up." He smiled and rose from his squat. "I sure as hell am glad I came out here."

"I am, too."

He surprised her by reaching out to touch her cheek lightly. A shiver of a different kind ran through her, but he dropped his hand swiftly. "Let's see if we can find where all these drafts are coming from."

The swift change left her off balance. After a moment she collected her scattered thoughts. It would have been so easy to just sink into the pleasure his lightest touch could cause her. "I looked and couldn't figure it out."

"As hard as it's blowing, it wouldn't take large chinks to create a problem. You might also have been losing some heat up the chimney pipe since you didn't have a fire, and then there's those windows. Single-paned. Not good." He paused. "I guess Winona was right."

"Was she? I haven't been following the weather."

"Out here you should. But yeah, this storm wasn't predicted by the meteorologists. My dad said they're busy trying to explain that mountains create their own weather."

"Do they?"

"Oh, yeah. But a storm like this?" He shook his head. "I need to be careful or I'm going to start believing in Winona."

She laughed. "Would that be so bad?"

"Terrible." He winked. "Okay, now for some more of that coffee and a hunt for chinks."

She was happy to refill his mug. It was such a little thing to do for the man who had come riding to her rescue. Worry about him being here for a few days settled onto the back burner for now. As long as they had impersonal subjects for discussion, she was safe. And her delight seemed to be overcoming her instinctive worries anyway. It was a happy change, as far as she was concerned. "What could we do about them anyway?" she asked. "I mean, to fill them?"

"Depends on how big they are. I could use all your socks. Or some of that caulking in my truck might be enough."

She glanced out the window again. "Won't it freeze out there?"

For once *he* was the one who appeared startled. "You're right. And the food. Okay, let me get that stuff safely stowed in here. I'm running ahead of myself."

More boxes appeared inside, some near the kitchen and stocked with canned and dried goods. He put a couple of tubes of caulking on the small table, then began to hunt around the cabin for where the cold air was getting in.

Meanwhile, the stove began to elevate the temperature, doing far better than the heater had.

He had no more luck than she. He finally pulled out a chair at the table, shucked his jacket and remarked, "Maybe it's just temperature differential. You do have those windows. They need thermal drapes."

"I didn't think of anything like that when I moved in."

His smile was crooked. "Of course not. It was June. But I'm through reorganizing your life. I'm surprised you haven't snapped at me yet. I'm sure you're perfectly capable of making your own decisions."

She sat across from him, wishing she was sure of that. "I don't know," she said finally. "There are a whole lot of things I never thought about when I came here. I just wanted to be here."

"God's country," he said quietly. Pivoting on his chair,

he reached for the coffeepot and topped off both their mugs. "As long as we have coffee…"

She laughed at that. "Who needs anything else, especially now that it's getting warm in here."

"Too warm?" he asked immediately.

"Maybe warm enough to ditch the sweater. That would be nice. But no, I'm not uncomfortable."

Then came one of those long silences that she dreaded. She realized in theory that people could be comfortable with silence, but for her those quiet spells had become fraught with threat. She didn't have the small talk; she couldn't summon some past memory to share with humor. She quite simply had little she dared to mention except the immediate. If the silence went on long enough, he might start asking questions she couldn't answer, just to chat.

But he leaned back, looking out the window at the blizzard that had cut off the world, seeming content to sip his coffee.

After a while he remarked, "Can I say I'm having a good time? I don't often get to relax like this."

"Working a ranch must be hard."

"It's certainly busy. You get used to the work at an early age, though. We're not gentlemen ranchers, but honest-to-goodness working cowboys. We do almost all of it."

She bit her lip, hesitating. It was hard when you weren't even sure what questions to ask. "The cattle? How do they get through something like this?"

He looked at her then. "They huddle together, we built windbreaks out of hay for them, and if we're lucky, most of them will make it, as long as it doesn't get too cold."

She pondered that, trying to imagine the loss in real terms. "So this storm could really cost you?"

"Yep." He paused. "We're luckier than most. Ranching is getting harder every year, but we have resources to fall back on. We'll be okay. But I admit, we don't like losing cattle. Every single one counts."

She eyed the storm outside the window, seeing it in a different way. Braden must be sitting there worried about his livelihood, yet he'd come here to bail her out. She couldn't imagine the cattle standing out in this, trying to stay out of the wind and keep as warm as possible. Yet, he seemed almost philosophical about it.

"You've faced this before?" she asked.

"We face winter every year. Other times it might be drought. We get by, though. Actually, we do better than just get by. We're lucky to be such a large operation."

She'd heard mentions around town that the Traub family did quite well with their ranching, although she had no idea exactly what that meant. Apparently, they were nowhere near dirt poor. That was, after all, a fairly new truck he drove.

She let her mind wander away from the threat the blizzard posed, deciding he had judged it from experience, and he didn't seem too awfully worried. Her stomach growled unexpectedly, and her cheeks heated. "Sorry, I haven't eaten yet. I'm a bad hostess. Would you like breakfast?"

"Just more coffee for now. I had breakfast right before I headed out here. You go ahead and eat."

While she prepared her egg and toast, he carried his mug over to the window and stared out into the blizzard. It gave her a nice view of his broad shoulders and narrow hips, and the opportunity to just gaze.

It struck her that he might be feeling caged at the moment. He must be a man used to spending the majority of his time outdoors, and right now he was trapped inside. He was also accustomed to working a lot, and he had not a thing to do here, really. He had done what he had come to do, and now he was a prisoner of the storm and these four walls.

And maybe he was worrying more than he let on. That storm out there was dangerous for man and beast alike.

She could think of no distraction to offer. She had no games lying around, no way to wile the time. There was just the two of them, and conversation, or silence. Given how she felt about conversation, silence seemed preferable.

But she wanted him to like her. A vain hope considering that if he found out the truth about her, he'd probably head the other direction as fast as he could. Still, it would be nice to make him smile, to be able to entertain him, to make him enjoy time with her.

To feel once again that she was truly worth something to someone. If she had ever felt that way. How would she know?

That damn wall in her memory reared up again, and she stared at its blank granite face. Blank, except for a name, a mountain and a pageant. It was a huge wall, and that was little enough to put on it.

"Winona wants to talk to you," he said, turning from the window.

Her heart skipped several beats, and for a second she felt lightheaded. "Why? I don't want to talk to her."

He half smiled. "I already figured that out. But I ran into her the other day, and she said she needed to talk to you. Nothing about why. Nothing about what. Winona can be the definition of cryptic. Regardless, if you don't want to talk to her, you'd better keep your distance."

"I don't like the way she makes me feel," Jenn admitted reluctantly. "It's kind of weird. Nobody's made me

feel like that before." At least not in the short period of
her life that she could remember.

"Maybe she just pulled lottery numbers out of the
thin air for you."

She gave a halfhearted laugh, but there was no way
on earth she could explain to herself why she reacted to
Winona the way she did. That sense of an electric shock.
An unreasoning fear, she supposed. But if she planned
on staying here, she doubted she could avoid the woman
forever.

Braden came her way and began to make a fresh pot
of coffee. Then he went to his jacket, which he'd hung
on one of the cabin's most useful items: a peg beside
the door.

"I have a deck of cards. Care to play?" He pulled out
a battered pack. "I can't guarantee you can't see through
them."

"Why not?" She wished her heartbeat would slow
down.

"You will never know how many poker games get
played around a campfire at night. Or on a long evening.
This is my lucky deck, though, so I won't replace it."

"Lucky deck?" she repeated, blinking, her anxiety
easing a bit. At least he wasn't going to keep talking
about Winona.

"Sure. I've cleaned out my brothers a few times with
it."

"Cleaned them out? For real money?"

He laughed. "No way. I have to see them often enough.
So I have a box of plastic chips in the truck. But we don't
have to play poker. Any game will do. We can keep track
of points if you have a pad and pencil."

The wind never stopped howling. The density of the
cabin walls toned it down some, but the keening was

still audible, and the way the windows rattled sometimes couldn't be ignored.

Braden was glad he was here. From what he'd seen, if the power went out, Jenn would have been in a world of hurt. He'd barely made it here as it was, a certain reck-lessness and determination drawing him over here in weather he would never have otherwise tried to drive through.

He even patted himself on the back for bringing out the deck of cards. He had the pleasure of seeing her se-riously relax, forgetting whatever those things were that sometimes disturbed or frightened her. She focused en-tirely on the games they played, and he was careful to direct his conversation mostly the same way.

They played hearts and spades, and finally he taught her seven-card stud. Poker wasn't the best game in the world with only two players, but she seemed to enjoy learning how it worked. If he'd had another deck of cards, he'd have suggested pinochle.

They lunched on the bread and cold cuts he'd brought with him, made even more coffee, and soon they were chatting and laughing, if not like old friends, certainly like comfortable card game buddies.

None of that answered his questions about her, but he figured now wouldn't be a good time to pry. If he upset her, she couldn't even throw him out.

He went outside to bring in some more wood, noting that the storm seemed to be worsening. Two-foot drifts had appeared against the cabin, and the sky hadn't light-ened one bit. If anything, the sky had darkened; the gray clouds seemed like a portent of worse to come.

When he'd finished bringing in the wood and checked the fire, he straightened to find her standing with her hands clasped, looking at him.

"When is this going to stop?" she asked. "I get that it could go on all day, but it seems to be getting worse. Is it?"

"Yeah, it is. We had more light a couple of hours ago. I think the clouds have thickened. As for when it'll be over, I don't know. Want me to call Winona?"

He'd meant it as a joke, but saw again that fear flicker across her face. He couldn't imagine why anyone should be afraid of the psychic. She was harmless; you could listen to her or not as you chose. Why should Jenn even care?

But clearly she did, and that heightened his curiosity even more. The woman was like a box of secrets, and every little thing whetted his appetite for more answers.

He'd noticed, for example, that when he occasionally had recalled childhood memories today, like jumping in the cattle pond only to come up so covered with muck, he'd needed to be hosed down in the barnyard, she hadn't volunteered a single story from her own childhood. Not one amusing memory. Not any kind of memory at all.

"I won't call Winona," he said after a moment. "I will note for the record that while she said this storm was coming, she didn't tell us a date. Now how could I ask her to know when it ends?"

A little laugh escaped her, and her tension fled. "Good point. But I kind of meant, you've lived here all your life. How long do these things usually last?"

"It varies. Are you tired of me already?" He was joking, but her response made it clear she hadn't taken it that way.

She stepped toward him, hand out. "No! Oh, no, Braden, this has been fun so far. And you came to my rescue."

He waved a hand. "Forget the rescue part. Just as long as I'm not overstaying my welcome."

"I don't think that could happen."

The words appeared to startle her as much as they did him. What was she saying? Should he move in closer? Did she want something more from him?

Before he could do a thing, the power went out. At once the cabin was concealed in dark shadows that danced in the red glow of the stove.

"Oh, man," she breathed.

"Well, now comes the fun," he said with deliberate cheer. "Might as well nest out here near the stove. I was getting tired of the table anyway."

She sighed. "So was I. I think I have some candles. And a flashlight."

"Well, we don't exactly need them right now. The stove is giving off enough light."

"Not if you want to play cards."

He tilted his head. "Do you?" Because he was getting the distinct impression that playing cards had taken some kind of pressure off her. That pressure interested him. Was she afraid of just having an ordinary conversation? Why in the world could that be?

"Not really. Not just yet," she said slowly.

Right then and there he made up his mind not to say anything much unless she initiated a conversation. One of these days he wanted to get to the root of whatever her problem was, but there was no reason to push.

"Well," she said after a moment, "I guess we could treat this like a camping trip."

She turned and went to pull the comforter off her bed, along with the pillows. She spread them on the floor in front of the stove, but not too close. Then she returned to a small closet and pulled out another comforter. "The floor is hard," she said by way of explanation.

Only if you wanted to sit on it, he thought. He took

one of the ancient armchairs, careful to leave her some unthreatening space. She even took the bright blue blanket she'd bought and spread it with the rest. Then she plopped down in the middle of the nest, her back to him.

He might as well have not even been there. It was as if she was shutting him out in some way. With anyone else he might have felt stung, but not with this woman. He was beginning to believe that her problems were huge and went deep.

All he knew was that he wished there was some damn way he could help her. It bothered him to see her troubled, to sense that she felt alone even among friends, to feel that she was frightened of something. But how could he ask? If he did, he wouldn't blame her for driving him out into the blizzard.

They were hardly acquainted, after all, and right now were sharing an intimacy that had been manufactured by the storm, not something they had built themselves.

An intimacy they would apparently never share as long as she kept her secrets. He rubbed his chin, staring at the back of her head, resisting an urge to sit down beside her and wrap her in his arms in the hope that an embrace might make her feel safer from whatever demon she harbored.

Another reason for her to kick him out, he thought ruefully.

Then she astonished him, leaving him to hold his breath and wait.

"Can you keep a secret?" she asked.

"From everyone?"

"Yes. From your family and everyone else. I don't want anybody to know."

"I can do that, unless you're about to tell me you're a bank robber."

Her laugh sounded almost bitter. "I can't stand it anymore," she said quietly. "I just can't. I'm all alone inside my head, damaged, afraid. You may as well know, since you're being so nice. I'm not normal. And after this you'll probably want nothing to do with me ever again."

"I can't imagine that."

She finally twisted on the blankets, looking at him. "You're attracted to me?"

He supposed it had been written all over him, and he wasn't ashamed that she knew. That's how men and women got together. Nature and all that. "Hell, yeah."

"Well, I'm attracted to you, too." She faced the stove again. "And nothing can ever come from it."

For some reason, his heart almost stopped. He'd expected a whole lot of things, but not her to turn him away before he'd even made a real approach. The idea pained him, although it seemed extreme considering the short time he'd known her. "Why? Are you married?"

"That's just it," she said finally, her voice sharpening and rising a bit. *"I don't know!"*

Chapter Seven

Braden didn't know how to react. He wanted to slide down beside her and hold her, but he feared that something important was happening inside her, something that shouldn't be interrupted. Her emotional earthquake was almost palpable to him, as dramatic as the storm that battered Rust Creek Falls.

He was in over his head; he knew that before she even began speaking. But he bit back any sound, any gesture, that might interrupt her. Whatever this was, she desperately needed it to happen.

"I haven't told my girlfriends," she said, her voice thin. "I haven't told anyone. I'm so ashamed."

"Of what?" he dared to ask quietly. Never would he tell her all the imaginings that popped into his head at that confession. The matters that might shame her created a long list, but certainly not what came out of her next.

"I have amnesia," she said, her voice breaking. "I don't know who I am. I don't remember a single thing before I woke up from a coma in the hospital four years ago. I don't even know what happened to me."

He saw her hand reach up to touch the back of her head, stroking something he couldn't see.

"I was found wandering without any identification. All I had were the clothes on my back and this necklace. God, Braden, even the doctors didn't really believe at first

that I couldn't remember anything of my past at all. Do
you know how rare that is?"

"No," he admitted. Inside he felt rocked to the core by
what she was telling him. It was as if everything he had
felt and noticed about her imploded until one great big
monolith in his mind covered it all. Her skittishness, her
lack of conversation, her occasional evasions... It was
enough to leave him stunned.

"I'm someone, obviously, but I don't know who. I've
been searching, and my search brought me here, but I
still don't know anything about who I was, what kind
of person I was. Or, like I said, whether I'm married.
Although I'm probably not because the cops hunted the
missing persons reports and I never came up. Whoever
I was apparently didn't make friends or have family."

He hesitated, sorrow replacing shock. "You can't be
sure."

"Of course I can't be sure. All I can be sure of is that
nobody gave enough of a damn to report me missing."

"Maybe you'd moved on for some reason, and they
didn't expect you to come back."

She swiveled her head, looking at him from the corner of her eye. "That's a kind explanation. The truth is
probably not as pretty. Part of me is desperate to recover
my past, and part of me is terrified of it. What if I don't
like the woman I used to be?"

"But you're the woman you are now," he argued quietly.

"Who is she? I don't know!"

"She's Jenn or Jennifer. You got that much, right?"

"Maybe." She pulled up her knees, resting her chin
on them, wrapping her arms around her legs. "How can
I be sure?"

"I don't know," he admitted. "But you seemed awfully certain when you told me. And then there was the

mountain. I don't think you could come from this town. By now someone would have recognized you, but there are other towns that mountain is visible from. Maybe we need to check them out."

"Or it could just resemble a mountain I used to know."

He fell silent for a while, but when she offered nothing more, he left his chair to sit beside her on the blankets. Hesitantly, he reached for her hand and was relieved when she didn't snatch it back. He squeezed it, holding it and caressing it gently with his fingers, clamping down on the desires she always evoked in him.

"This must be enough to make you crazy sometimes," he remarked.

"Sometimes I think I *am* crazy. I just know… Well, I don't know a whole lot. I feel like I'm running in circles in a hamster wheel, looking for a way off. I've had a few flashes that seemed to come from my past, but I don't know whether to trust them."

"Why not?"

"Because that big empty hole has been there so long now that I may be filling it with wishful thinking."

God, he hadn't even thought of that. Not that he'd had a whole lot of time to think of anything yet. He still felt rocked back on his heels by her revelation; he ached for the pain she must endure. But there was one thing he could be utterly frank about. "I can't imagine it, Jenn. I just simply can't imagine what it must be like for you."

"Nobody can," she admitted. Her chin still rested on her knees. "I don't even know if I can explain it. It's like there's this huge, blank wall in my mind, and I can't reach anything that's behind it. Sometimes, for brief periods, I forget it. I'm just in the moment. Then something will happen to remind me. A question I can't answer."

He turned it round in his mind. "So that's why you sometimes seem evasive."

"Yeah. Because I just don't know. And I get so tired of having to slip away from questions I should be able to answer, or come up with something noncommittal enough that I don't get asked more questions."

He gave her hand another gentle squeeze. "Has it occurred to you that maybe folks would understand better than you think? I'm not running. Maybe you noticed."

"Where can you run to in the middle of this storm?"

That ignited a spark of anger in him. "I wouldn't run if it was a clear day out there. Let's get that straight from the start. I'm not sitting here thinking about me. I'm thinking about you."

She turned her head, until her cheek rested on her knee, and looked at him. "You're a very nice man, Braden Traub. Look at me. I'm not normal."

"What's normal?" His voice held a slight edge of anger. "Why do you even ask yourself that? Why torment yourself? You have a big enough problem already without walking around feeling abnormal."

She lifted her head. "You can't possibly think total amnesia is normal!"

He was relieved to see that flare in her. "Think about all the soldiers coming back from war with traumatic brain injuries. They've changed, but just because they've changed, that doesn't mean they're not normal. They're normal *for what they have been through*."

"That's a false argument," she said and averted her face.

"No, it's not. It's the truth. Normal is a relative thing. Do yourself a favor and recognize that much, at least. Then you can get on with life without feeling like you can't possibly find a place to belong."

Her head pivoted sharply around toward him. "How do you know that?"

"It's a feeling I get from you. You don't feel you belong, and you're afraid you never will. Tell me that isn't true."

He watched her open her mouth, as if she wanted to respond, then she slumped again, burying her face against her knees, curling into a tight ball. He wanted to pry her out of that ball, to help her relax, to let her know that she really *wasn't* alone unless she chose to be.

But he was well and truly in over his head and he knew it. He thought about what little he'd seen of her, and realized that even though she was surrounded by girlfriends sometimes, she didn't really let them close to her. It was as if she walked in an invisible bubble, unable to reach out, unable to be reached.

He wished he had some magic wand to wave, some perfect words to speak. Something to reach her, to let her know it was safe to let someone inside her shell.

Her obvious retreat frightened him, though. He felt as if she were slipping away, and that if he didn't stop her withdrawal, she might just disappear like a mist.

Shoving himself to his feet so he couldn't do something stupid like grab her and force a hug on her, he paced the small cabin. The storm that raged outside didn't hold a candle to the one she faced inside, he guessed. He couldn't imagine all that she endured and would continue to endure.

But he had to get through to her, to make her understand that her loss of memory wasn't some kind of scarlet letter. Whoever she had been before, she needed to understand that people liked the person she was now. He'd seen it in a group of women he admired, women who called her friend and had invited her into their circle.

In himself. He hadn't come barreling out here to help

someone he didn't like. He'd known he was going to be stuck here until this storm cleared and the roads opened up again. He'd *wanted* to go through this blizzard here, with her.

But he was afraid he would scare her if he told her that, even though it might reassure her that someone truly wanted to be with her. Damn, he wished he understood better, but there was only one way that would happen. She had to talk, and right now she resembled a clam that had pulled back into its shell.

"Jenn?"

"Hmm?" The sound was muffled.

"Want some more coffee?"

She lifted her head a little. "I think I'm wired enough."

"Or maybe not. Milk? Something to eat? A lesson in how to cook on the woodstove?" He didn't care what pulled her back to him. Hell, he'd go out into the blizzard and build a snowman for her amusement right outside the window.

"I'm sorry," she said after a moment. "I don't know why I dumped on you."

"Don't be sorry. I'm glad I'm here. I'm ready to listen to anything you want to say. But I'm trying really hard not to push you."

At last she sighed and let go of her crouch. Moving a bit gingerly, as if she had stiffened, she straightened out her legs, then stood up. "I'm not being much of a hostess."

"I don't remember being an invited guest. I'm not looking for a hostess anyway."

She turned slowly in place and tried to give him a smile. The expression was wan, and her eyes were pinched, even a little frightened.

"Relax," he said after a moment. "I still like you, I'm

still attracted to you, and frankly I don't care who you might have been before. I like who you are now."

Exactly the wrong thing to say. He saw it instantly, but it was too late to swallow the words. He wanted to kick his own butt.

"What if I remember? What if I'm really some awful person?"

At least he could answer that one. "You're not an awful person right now. If you *used* to be one, that doesn't mean you have to be one again."

Well, at least that appeared to be the right answer. She relaxed visibly and took a step toward him. "I am a little hungry," she admitted. "For a light snack."

"I'm sure I brought some of those. The Traub household can't function without easily portable snacks."

He checked the boxes he'd brought in and came up with a package of pretzels. "These look good?"

"Yummy. I'll get a bowl."

"Good heavens, you don't eat out of the bag?" He was teasing, and it pleased him when her smile became more natural.

"Not when I can reach a bowl."

"My mother would love you. She's death on bag eaters."

Jenn laughed, and the tension eased out of the cabin. No telling for how long, but he was willing to bide his time and see what came down the pike. Given the weather out there, he was fairly certain they would be here for a few days. Long enough for her to confide in him again as long as he was careful.

Because he really *did* want to know more about her, about the time since her injury, since she couldn't recall anything before that. It occurred to him that she must be a really amazing person, to have faced all that and somehow come through it until she found a place and friends here in the middle of virtual nowhere. Hell of a risk, he thought, given that it would have been easier for her to remain anonymous in a big city. Around here, everyone knew who had sneezed and when.

They once again sat at the table, the glow of the stove barely reaching them. She seemed to have little interest in light at the moment, and he supposed she felt safer right now in the shadows. He wished she'd just say so, but what she had confided already was huge. He hoped she didn't wonder if she'd made a mistake.

He peered into her darkened fridge and pulled out two soft drinks. "They're getting warm," he said as he placed the cans on the table."

That made her laugh quietly. "You can always stick them outside the front door."

"I'm already using Mother Nature's freezer. There are steaks in my truck, and some burgers."

Her eyes widened. "Did you overlook anything?"

"Hey, I like my food. I hope you do, too."

"Food and I get along pretty well."

Safe ground. He was relieved to see her cheering up, but hoped that didn't mean the end of her confidences. He glanced at the deck of cards that had gotten them through the early part of the day, then dismissed them. No more diversions. Just him, her and whatever she wanted to talk about.

But she didn't say anything for a while, so he decided to open the can of worms again. "You know, this is like a mystery."

"What?" She looked uncertain.

"Yeah, as in 'Who is that gorgeous woman and how did she get here?'"

She could have reacted in a lot of ways, but this time

she didn't choose to dance around. "You really want to know?"

"Everything you're willing to tell me. I'm interested. I like you. I kind of feel like now we're in this together."

"I wouldn't ask that of anyone," she said, her face shadowing a bit.

"You didn't ask. I'm volunteering."

She studied his face as if trying to read him. He waited patiently, figuring this was something that had to come in her own way in her own time.

"It's been hard," she admitted finally. "The worst was at first. I was so terrified, I can't even tell you. I had no past and no memory older than a few days. They gave me some therapy to help me deal, and then told me my memory might return spontaneously, all at once or just some bits and pieces from time to time."

"Or never at all."

"They didn't like to mention that. Anyway, I'm grateful that I didn't forget a lot of things, apparently. I can still do most of the things I need to do."

"Like walk and talk."

At that she actually laughed, a small one. "And dress myself, and cook."

"I'm glad you remembered how to make that chicken we had the other night. Fabulous."

Her smile widened a hair. "Folks were good to me, Braden. They had to get me a whole identity so I could work, then the psychologist encouraged me to find a job that didn't make me feel threatened. It wasn't easy without references, but I found one working in a small dress shop. Little by little I gained at least some confidence. I could use a cash register, I could count change, I could pass a few easy pleasantries. But I also felt overwhelmed. I still hate to be in large groups. I still feel uncomfortable with most conversation unless it's about some immediate matter. I have no answers to common questions, so I'd like it if people didn't ask them. But of course they do. It's natural. Like at the pageant, the girls were talking about family holiday traditions, and they wondered about mine. All I could say was we didn't have any."

She fell silent, clasping her hands on the table in front of her.

"I'm still trying to imagine it," he said presently. "I just can't wrap my head around what it would be like not to be able to remember my family, or our holidays or the dumb things my brothers and I did."

"And I can't imagine what it's like to remember all of that."

"You must feel awfully adrift."

"I do. Even now, with some experience and memories under my belt, I'm still not sure who I am, where I've been or anything else. And I'm scared of something else," she admitted.

"What's that?" He leaned toward her, intent on every word.

"That I could wake up again without any memory." Her voice stretched thin. "It happened once. I can't quite believe it won't happen again."

That was too much for him. Way too much. That this woman was actually sitting here, having found the courage to come all the way to Montana in search of something she couldn't even identify, awed him. "You've got more courage than anyone I've ever known."

Then he was up out of his chair and around the table, drawing her up until he held her tightly against him, burying his face in her hair, feeling every delicious curve of hers against him, but aware beyond anything of her amazing courage and determination.

He'd found the qualities in her that he'd seldom seen in anyone else.

She didn't push him away. After a momentary stiffening of surprise, she melted into him as if his embrace filled some aching, empty place inside her.

Maybe it did, he thought as he held her. Jenn was the most alone person he had ever met.

Braden's arms felt so strong, warm and reassuring. Jenn allowed herself to relax into them, to lean against him and close her eyes. He hadn't run, hadn't rejected her. Instead, he had reached out to offer the most basic comfort in the world, a hug.

She didn't even know when last she had been hugged. If she let herself think about it, she'd get on that stupid hamster wheel again, and she didn't want to do that right now.

She wanted to pretend she was an ordinary woman with an unshadowed life, resting in the arms of a lover. She wanted to give in to all the attraction she felt for this man, to find out—maybe for the first time in her life, but certainly for the first time in *this* life—what it was like to make love with a man. And not just any man, but this one. From the start she'd felt the longing for him, no matter how hard she tried to hide it from herself. Braden called to her in the most elemental way possible.

She wanted to throw caution and worry to the winds and lie in this man's arms. Tentatively, she turned her face up to look at him. Her heart nearly stopped when she saw an answering fire blazing in his warm brown gaze.

"I could," he said quietly, "make love to you right this instant. I want to. But would that be right? Are you really ready for that? Because I don't want to be just an escape."

The justice of his concern felt like lead in her heart.

Escape right now would be easy, and it was certainly tempting. But it would only be a temporary escape, and in fairness to him, she couldn't use him that way.

"So where do we go from here?" she murmured.

"You could tell me more about what you do remember since you woke up. What you've been up to. How you got here. We could just talk, Jenn. I'm old enough to understand that hormones are no substitute for getting to know someone."

"But you can't really know me."

"You think not? I already know how brave you are. Suppose you tell me how resourceful you are, as well."

With that, the escape hatch closed. She sighed, backed away then curled up on the blankets again, sitting cross-legged this time. He paused to put another log on the fire then came to sit on the floor beside her.

He finally pushed her a little when her silence lingered. "Pretend you don't have that blank wall on much of your past. Tell me how you got by after you awoke. I'm really curious how you came to be here."

She rubbed her free hand along her thigh, trying to ease the tension that had returned. She'd already told him the worst, that she didn't know who she used to be. How hard could it be to discuss the time since she left the hospital? She'd certainly been over it in her head enough times, hoping some little clue would leap out at her.

"Abbreviated version," she said finally. "I told you they helped me with some therapy, that they managed to give me an identity, and my psychologist found me my first job. With a friend of hers. Did I tell you that?"

"Not that it was her friend."

"It was. Nobody else would have taken me on, I'm sure. I had no past, no references, no prior job experience, at least to my knowledge. So her friend gave me a

part-time position. I'd probably still be there except..."
After a moment she just blurted it out. "I was restless.
Very restless. I kept feeling like I was in the wrong place.
Something wasn't right. It was too warm. There wasn't
enough snow. So I started moving around. Kind of a roll-
ing stone. I managed to find temporary and part-time
jobs until I wound up working in that antiques store in
Worcester."

"And that's where things came to a head?"

"In a way. I started dreaming about snow and mountains, and I knew I still wasn't in the right place. Hilda,
the lady who owned the antiques store, got most of my
story from me, and I guess she felt some sympathy. She
told me to go to the library and start looking around. She
said it would be easier and safer to search for places on
the web, rather than packing up and moving yet again."

She glimpsed his nod from the corner of her eye. "And
that brought you here?"

"Partly. I mean, I realized that every time pictures
of the Rocky Mountains would come up, I felt drawn to
them. But the Rockies are a big place. I needed something narrower. That's when Fred Krieg came into the
shop one day and noticed my necklace. He was fascinated
by it, told me he was a coin specialist, and he wanted to
know all about it."

She fell silent again, moving back in time, into that as-
tonishing moment of pure luck. Finally, she spoke again.
"I told him all I knew was it was an heirloom, but I didn't
know from where. Well, that really roused his curiosity.
Next thing I knew, he asked me to come to his shop so
he could investigate it."

"And you went?"

"I went. It took him a few weeks, but finally he told

me the last owner of these coins had lived in Montana. That's all he could tell me."

Braden stirred. "Really? Not a name? Nothing? I'd think that would be some kind of public record or something."

"They were insured. That's how he found out where the last owner was from, but insurance companies, according to him, don't divulge private information. Not a chance he could find the name or even the city of the owner. He said we were lucky to get what we had."

"Wow."

She clearly remembered her despair at the news. It sounded so clinical, but she had placed so much hope in his figuring out who had owned that necklace that she had felt nearly crushed by the dead end. Her whole life, she had thought at the time, was one big dead end. The news had kept her away from Fred's shop, because she couldn't stand another disappointment. Another lead that went nowhere, not that she had had many leads.

She'd haunted the library computers and found Lissa Roarke's blog about Rust Creek Falls. "I started reading Lissa's blog. I knew this wasn't exactly the right place, but it seemed like as good a place as any to start. I just didn't know how I was going to do it. Every time I had changed jobs, it just made getting the next job harder."

"I guess it would."

She shook her head. "I knew I was coming to some kind of end. I had to take one last step, and had become a little obsessed with this place. I read about your flood last year, about all the people who were coming to help with the recovery effort, and I thought I wouldn't stand out too much, and maybe I'd figure out something. With all the people coming to help, maybe someone would know me."

"I think you stood out a little more than you expected."

A short laugh escaped her. "Maybe. Lots of new people around. That's why I joined the Newcomers Club. I hoped maybe I'd meet someone who would have an answer. Instead, I just got a lot of questions. But anyway, I finally went back to Fred, asked him how much he'd give me for one of my coins. He was awfully generous, or at least it felt like it. He gave me my seed money to come out here and stay awhile. So here I am."

He stroked the back of her hand then astonished her by lifting her onto his lap, facing forward so that her back rested against his chest. He ignored the inevitable throbbing need she caused in him, because comforting her was far more important.

"I say again, you are one courageous, resourceful woman. I don't know many who would have moved all the way out here with so little to go on."

"It was *all* I had to go on. It was my last hope. I'm not brave."

"I disagree."

Then, to her amazement, she felt him press his face to the back of her head. All of a sudden, before she could truly enjoy the sensation, she felt him stiffen.

"Is that a scar?"

Her hand flew up instinctively and touched the narrow ridge on the back of her head. "Yes," she said quietly, almost choking on her hammering heart. "That's what caused it all."

He lifted his hands, loosened the band holding her ponytail, then gently parted her hair with his fingertips. Shivers of pleasure ran through her at the gentle touches. "God," he said quietly. "Whatever happened, it must have been bad. What *did* happen?"

"No one knows what caused it, crime or accident. I

was found wandering with a skull fracture. Bleeding inside my head. I'm lucky to be alive."

"You certainly are. But you don't feel that way, do you?"

"Sometimes. I mean, sometimes it overwhelms me, you know? I could be dead, and I wouldn't even know."

He startled her with a laugh. After a moment she realized how that had sounded, and a laugh escaped her, too.

"Okay, that was stupid," she admitted.

"I didn't say that. It just sounded funny. But you meant something else, didn't you? How many times did you wish you *had* died?"

"More than once, right afterward. It doesn't happen anymore. But for a while I thought it would have been easier."

"Yeah, I can see that. I really can." He dropped his hands. "Sorry I messed up your hair."

But she wasn't. This time when he leaned into her, she could feel the warmth of his lips on that scar. He was kissing it! Warmth spilled through her, followed by a sudden need so searing that her insides tightened.

She realized that in that instant if there was one thing she wanted as much as to know who she really was, it was Braden. She ached to feel his hands on her, to feel him inside her, to know what it was like.

"Braden," she said, her voice so thick, his name almost didn't come out.

"I feel you," he murmured.

His choice of words at once seemed odd and yet right. He wanted to know her first, but he knew essentially all there was to know about her, the pathetic story of her search for self and place. Maybe part of that search could be answered right now with him. Maybe she was afraid of knowing any more about her past, but she wasn't afraid of this.

She wanted him, and for once she wasn't afraid of what she didn't know. Wasn't afraid of what she might learn about herself, or discover that she didn't know. Being held like this was heaven, and if he refused to take it any further, she promised herself she wouldn't despair…but she knew she would. Driven by obsession all this time, she was now driven by something else even stronger, and she loved the feeling. The need. The release that need gave her.

To just be a woman at her most basic seemed like the greatest gift on the planet. To stop being guarded, to stop censoring herself, to stop fearing. To just *be*.

It might not be the best rationale in the world, but that didn't matter. She didn't want a rationale. She wanted Braden. All of him. However he chose to share himself with her. She had leaped past all the inhibitions she had developed because she wanted him more than anything on this planet.

Her heartbeat had grown heavy, and her body throbbed in time with it. She hadn't dreamed she could get so aroused so fast. Nor was she going to question it. Not now. In the thrall of these moments, nothing else mattered.

The wait seemed endless, though it couldn't have been but a minute. Then he lifted her from his lap. Just as she started to crash, thinking he was going to reject her, he lay down beside her on the blankets. Propped on his arm, he leaned over her, cupping her face with his hand, catching a few stray tendrils of her hair.

Outside the storm still raged. Dimly she heard the wind keen, and almost jumped when something thudded against the side of the cabin.

"Easy," he murmured. "The storm's just reaching a peak now."

She was reaching a peak, she realized, and hanging on tenterhooks now, wondering what would happen next. He might just be letting her down gently. Or… Anticipation leaped in her, deepening the demanding throb inside her.

"Have you done this before?"

The question was asked kindly, but it jarred her, and for a moment the heavy deepening pool of desire faded. "I don't know." The words came out stretched as fine as thin wire, because it was so painful to have to keep facing the fact that she didn't know *anything* about herself. Not even this.

"It's okay," he said, still cradling her cheek. He bent and kissed her ever so lightly on her lips. "I just want to know where I'm at. So I guess I shouldn't play the caveman and give in to my wildest impulses just now."

Her eyelids fluttered, then opened wide. "Really? I don't know what you're talking about, not really, but it sounds good."

He laughed quietly. "We'll get to that. But for right now this is a first time, most especially for you. But for me, too."

"How can it be for you?"

"Because I've never made love to Jennifer before."

That eased her apprehension in ways she couldn't begin to describe. She wondered if this man had even a vague idea how large was his innate kindness.

"You're sure about this?" he asked. "I know I'm sure. I've been craving you for what seems like forever. But…"

A new kind of courage seemed to fill her. She lifted a hand and pressed her fingers to his lips, silencing him. "I'm sure. I *need* this."

* * *

Maybe she did, he thought as he bent his head and kissed her, taking her more deeply this time. Some corner of his mind warned him that unlike his past girlfriends, this time he was wading into deep emotional waters, and not just because of her problem. Thing was, he wanted her, but somehow he had come to care for her. Something about her seemed like a piece made to fit him, emotionally.

That was a bigger danger to him than sex. Sexual attraction eased eventually, as he'd discovered, while emotional connections stayed forever. But he also knew that dangers might await her in this. It might stir memories, or reactions for reasons she couldn't remember, and they might not be good ones. She was walking into uncharted territory, and even as his body pounded and throbbed with hunger for her, he knew he had to keep at least a corner of his mind in gear, to be aware of her reactions.

Well, it was a good idea anyway. One that rapidly faded as her arms wound around him, as her lips opened to his tongue, as her body arched in response as if she were already almost there.

"Damn, I hate clothes," he muttered. They were both swaddled in them. He was surprised when she laughed in response, and encouraged, he struggled to his feet and pulled her up.

"Let's get rid of them, right now. All of them. Game?"

Sleepy-eyed, smiling faintly, she nodded. "Cut me loose, Braden."

Wow, what an invitation. The shreds of his self-control were steadily snapping like rubber bands pulled too tight. Pounding need dominated him, and from what he could see, her, as well.

"Hurry," she said thickly. "Now. Please, now!"

Gentlemen first. He stripped quickly, cussing once at his boots, then stood before her as naked as the day he was born. His erection, freed of confinement, only throbbed harder.

Some part of him expected her to turn tail, but he waited as her amazing blue eyes wandered over him, as her breaths quickened, as her eyelids drooped. The instant her hands reached for the bottom of her sweater to pull it up, he became galvanized. Good intentions flew out the window.

He ached for her, and to hell with taking it easy. She was going to get him however passion demanded. If that wasn't going to work for her, best to know it now.

He stepped toward her, pushing her hands aside, and ripped the sweater off her. The fleece shirt followed quickly, revealing a surprisingly simple bra that cradled full breasts. Then her jeans and boots, another cuss word there, until she stood before him in her plain white underwear.

He filled his eyes with her, admiring her gentle curves, from breast to belly to thigh. Made for a man's hands, made for *his* hands.

"You're perfect," he mumbled, but speech was rapidly escaping him. Slow? No way. It couldn't be slow now.

Nor did she seem to want it. With her own hands she released her bra, allowing her breasts to spill free. Not too full, but fuller than he expected with pebbled pink nipples that begged for his mouth. Dropping to his knees, he tugged down her panties with his hands while finding her breast with his mouth. The groan that escaped her as he drew her nipple into him goaded him even more.

Her hands clutched his head, pulling him even closer, filling him with triumphant pleasure. She was with him.

All awareness of everything except this woman and the pleasures she offered flew from his mind.

She wanted loving, and he wanted to give it. All the loving he was capable of.

He gripped her hips as she groaned again, keeping his mouth latched to her breast. He sucked hard, loving the little sounds she made, then managed to pull back enough to move to her other breast. More groans. He felt her legs tremble, then almost without warning, she was on her knees facing him.

"Braden…" His name escaped her on a shuddery sigh, the most beautiful sound in the world. He caught her behind the knees and lowered her to the tangled blankets and clothing. Straddling her, he began to explore her with his mouth, struggling to hold back the urge to just enter her, claim her, make her his.

Propped on an elbow, he trailed kisses over her breasts and belly while his hand stole downward and found the cleft between her legs.

A cry escaped her, and she bucked upward, letting him know she was ready. Truly ready.

Too fast. The thought zipped across his mind, ephemeral as fog. It didn't slow him down. They were already at the top of the mountain, and ready to tumble over the edge.

He put a knee between her legs. At once she opened herself, spreading her legs, inviting him inside. Then the next knee. He looked down and saw her dewy core, open and ready for him, swollen with the passion that had built as fast as the damn storm outside.

He couldn't wait. For absolutely the first time in his adult life, Braden Traub lost his self-control. Completely and utterly.

Forgetting everything but the demands of their bodies, he found her opening and pressed into her. He barely noticed an instant of resistance inside her, then he was fully sheathed in her hot, wet depths. They were one.

Her legs lifted, winding around his as if she wanted him even closer. He obliged, burrowing as deeply as he could, his entire body throbbing in time to his strong, deep thrusts. She rose to meet him, fingers digging into his shoulders, legs locking him in place.

He flexed again and again, driving into her as if every answer in the universe awaited him there. When he felt her jerk and stiffen, felt the shudder run through her, heard the cry escape her, he let go and jetted into her until he felt he had emptied even his soul.

Dimly he knew he'd just gone somewhere he'd never gone before.

Then he collapsed on her, welcomed by her arms and legs, filled with her heady scent, filled with a need to never let go of this miracle.

Chapter Eight

Braden had no idea how long they lay like that. Eventually, reality began to pierce the beautiful bubble of hazy satisfaction. The storm still howled, and he felt grateful for its fury, because it had cut them off. Then he noticed the fire was dying, probably because the winds outside were sucking air up the chimney and causing it to burn faster. He needed to deal with that.

But mostly he noticed Jenn, curled in his arms like a trusting kitten. He reached out to pull a corner of blanket over her, and wondered if he really needed to move at all. Freezing to death in her arms didn't seem like the worst fate in the world.

But reality refused to back off. Brain cells, drugged by pleasure, began to flip back into action. He raised a heavy arm and tipped her face so that he could look at her.

"How are you?" he asked. Because he had a dim memory of something that now, and only now, shook him to his core.

"I am wonderful," she said softly but firmly then smiled. "You?"

"Fantastic. I don't want to move. But the fire..."

"Can wait another minute," she insisted, burrowing her face into his shoulder.

"Well, it could but... Jenn...I think that was really your first time. And I was so out of control."

"Hush," she said. "No apologies. It was perfect. Never apologize for something so good."

"But I must have hurt you…"

"Not enough to notice." Then she stirred, tipping her head to look at him. "I'm glad you were my first, that my first was so awesome."

A caveman-like impulse brought a smile to his face. He could have pounded his chest. "Really?"

"Really. Actually, if I ever learn any more about who I am, I'm glad it won't be that."

He turned that around. "So one less thing to worry about?"

"Yes. And one more thing to celebrate."

He could deal with that. In fact, he *liked* it. Swooping in, he stole another kiss. "So much for my self-control. I intended slow, easy, careful…"

A little laugh escaped her. "That can wait. This was perfect. Absolutely perfect." Then she surprised him by rolling away, revealing her full naked beauty, and flinging her arms up. "Damn, I am so *happy*!"

He suspected there was little enough of that in her life. Giving it to her made him feel as tall as the mountains. "You're good for my ego."

"Unlike your brothers," she said tartly.

He chuckled. "They're not so bad."

"Maybe not. I don't really know them. They don't all live here anymore, right?"

"Not all of them do anymore. Forrest and Clay live in Thunder Canyon with their wives and kids."

"So really you do most of the ranching by yourself."

"Mostly it's me. The others pitch in when they can, to help Mom and Dad out."

"No wonder you're so busy." She closed her eyes a

moment. "Thunder Canyon. I like the way that sounds. It kind of rolls on the tongue."

"Have you been there?"

"Not yet."

"We'll have to remedy that."

He linked his hand with hers, waiting, but when she said no more, he sat up. "I've got to take care of that fire. And I don't know about you, but I'm getting really hungry. Once I get the fire going, I'll cook us a meal. Okay?"

Her eyes popped open, and she smiled. "Okay. The rest of the world can go hang for now."

"You bet it can. I'm so glad Winona was right about this storm."

"So am I," she admitted, and for once he didn't see tension in her when he mentioned the psychic. "I could melt into a puddle."

"Not yet, we'll do that later."

Her laugh followed him as he forced himself to leave their little nest and hunt up his jeans and boots. As soon as his bottom half was safely covered, he helped her wrap herself in her new blue blanket and move back to a chair. "I don't want any sparks to reach you."

He moved everything else well away from the stove then opened the door to put another couple of logs in. The cabin *was* getting colder, he noticed. Either the wind was sucking all the heat up the chimney pipe, or this structure wasn't as good an insulator as he would have thought.

She surprised him with her next question. "Do you think Homer is okay?"

"He's no fool, crazed though he may seem. He knows he's welcome at the community church, and the pastor said he'd already gotten a cot for Homer. I'm certain he's there, and the pastor will make sure he has food."

He sat back on his heels as he closed the stove door

and peered at her over his shoulder. "You worry about others, don't you?"

"Of course. Who wouldn't?"

He turned his attention back to the logs, waiting for the moment when flames would seem to emerge from them, letting him know they'd caught. "Some wouldn't," he said. "You meet them every so often."

Staring into the fire, waiting for the coals to ignite the logs, he sorted through everything Jenn had shared with him that day. She had acted almost as if she thought she was protecting him by spilling the truth about her amnesia, exposing to him just how defective she was. Far from making him think of her as deeply flawed, however, he found himself full of a desire to give her back something, so that she could find joy in life again. He understood her fear of discovering that the truth about herself might be hideous, but he'd seen enough of her to guess with fair certainty that she'd never been an ugly person. Oh, anyone could be awful at times, but this woman didn't seem to have a mean bone in her body. Plenty of scared ones, but no mean ones.

For some reason, she seemed to trust him. Why? Because he hadn't flown the coop when she told him about her amnesia? That was little to go on. Maybe she had become trusting out of necessity. How else could you get on with anything when you had no memory?

As the logs started to catch, he realized he'd reached a decision. He was going to move heaven and earth to find out why Jenn had chosen this part of the planet to continue her search for her past. And if that meant bringing Winona Cobbs to her, then he'd do it.

But he wasn't going to tell her about it. She'd raise a ruckus, and he'd rather deal with that once Winona had seen her. Once he found out why Winona wanted to see her. That storm outside had helped make a kind of believer out of him. Or, maybe, Winona had learned something about Jenn's past by other means. Either way, the psychic didn't usually demand to see anyone, so she must know something.

If nothing else, it would be a good starting point.

Brushing his hands on his pants, he stood. "Dang, you can sit and watch a fire for hours without moving."

"Mesmerizing," Jenn agreed.

He turned and saw her wrapped in her blue blanket. Some of the uncertainty had returned, and it was his fault. He must have appeared to be ignoring her, and right now the least little thing would seem huge.

After all, she'd just lost her virginity, and could have no way to be sure how much she had thrilled him and pleased him. A smile began to play about his mouth as he thought about all the ways he could reassure her.

Then his stomach growled loudly. He was relieved when she laughed. "Feed yourself," she said.

"I'm gonna feed both of us, lady. Just you watch."

Curled up the soft wool of the blue blanket, Jenn felt almost decadent. Naked beneath the blanket, she was swaddled in warmth and comfort, and Braden refused any help as he sorted through her fridge and the supplies he had brought and began to manufacture a meal for them.

Her entire body still tingled with pleasure and newfound knowledge. Effortlessly, her mind summoned their lovemaking, bringing along with it the memories of sensations, sounds, scents, until the ache began to build in her again. She seemed to have developed an instant addiction to Braden, and while she knew it might lead to nothing—in fact, probably would lead to nothing, given her amnesia—for right now she didn't care. For right now the storm sealed them in a perfect cocoon.

Looking out the window at a world darkened by heavy clouds and hidden behind whirling curtains of white, she felt again her love of winter. Why winter drew her, she had no idea, of course, but draw her it did, and this storm seemed like an answer to a craving almost as deep in her as the craving she now felt for Braden.

Snowy mountains, that dangerous weather outside… she had been hunting for them as much as she had been hunting for her past. Somehow, she and the winter were linked, and she wondered if she would ever know why. But maybe there was no link at all, simply a love of the wild forces of nature.

Drawing her knees up to her chin, cuddling herself inside the blanket, she watched the snow and felt truly at home with it. At home, too, with the fire burning nearby, casting its flickering, ruddy glow over everything. She knew this the way she had known that mountain. At some level out of conscious reach, this was all part of her.

Braden carried a frying pan and the coffeepot to the woodstove, adjusted the vent and announced, "You had some eggs, so rather than let them spoil, we're going to have loaded scrambled eggs. It'll be ready fast, because this stove is hot."

"You could use the propane and have some control," she reminded him.

He arched a brow at her. "What? And give up my sturdy, reliable woodsman image? I think not. However, if I burn the eggs…"

Another laugh escaped her. He took her to a place where laughter was possible. "Then we eat something else?"

"Precisely. As in canned baked beans." He began to

use a spatula to keep the eggs moving in the pan. "What would you have done if you hadn't found out about your necklace, or run into Lissa's blog?"

She didn't want all that to intrude, but there was no escaping it. She couldn't hide in this private little moment forever. Of course he had questions, and now she felt she owed it to him to answer them. "I don't know. I was thinking about going to Canada."

"Really? Why? Do you feel like you're Canadian?"

"I don't know. I just knew the winters in Worcester weren't bad enough, and the mountains weren't high enough."

He waved briefly toward the window. "I give you a winter, madam. How does it feel?"

"Perfect, actually."

"I'm not sure everyone would agree with you." He pulled the pan off the top of the stove. "Stay where you are. I'll bring you a plate." Just then the coffee started to perk.

She took the opportunity to tuck the blanket under her arms, covering herself decently while leaving her shoulders bare. Part of her found this act of modesty amusing, but another part insisted that one didn't eat while naked.

Apparently, Braden agreed, because he returned with his shirt back on and offered her one of the two plates he held. Then out of his breast pocket he pulled a couple of forks. "I couldn't find the napkins."

"I use paper towels." And few enough of them.

"A woman after my own heart. Never could understand why I needed different paper to wipe my mouth from the paper I used to wipe up a spill."

"Cuz your mouth is special?"

In an instant the air seemed to leave the room. He stood stock-still, but all of a sudden his brown eyes appeared to blaze like the fire behind him. "Keep talking that way, and we'll both go hungry."

"Tempting," she admitted, but as if to disagree, her stomach rumbled, making her flush.

"Food first," he announced in response. The coffee was perking faster, and he went over to peer at the little glass knob on the top. "Almost ready."

He left his plate on the small table between their chairs and returned with mugs. "Dig in, Jenn. I hate cold scrambled eggs."

They were excellent scrambled eggs, still moist and full of bits of green pepper and onion she'd had, even some ham he had rustled up from somewhere. She complimented him between mouthfuls.

"Having to cook over a campfire and eat your own cooking has its rewards," he said, a twinkle in his eyes. "If you're still hungry after this, I'll make some trail toast."

"What's that?"

"Slabs of buttered bread browned on the stove. Or over a fire."

"Oh, yum." But it wasn't toast she was thinking of as she spoke. No, she was looking at him and drinking him in with her eyes as if he were nectar and she a bee. Behind him, through the window, the storm raged, and the day began to darken even more. She wanted that storm to go on forever.

He brought them both mugs of coffee then set the pot on the flange in front of the stove door. He hadn't tucked his shirt in yet, and she enjoyed watching him as he carried his mug to the window and looked out.

"How come you've never married?" she asked. "It seems impossible to believe that no one snatched you up by now."

He laughed. "A few tried. I tried a few times. It didn't work out. I finally figured out that attraction is great, but it's not enough. You have to really like a person, too. Like my parents. If they weren't best friends, I doubt they'd have been able to weather all these years together."

"So you think being best friends is important?"

"I think it's the most important part. Love is a hell of a lot more than great sex."

She liked that. A whole lot. Whoever got Braden Traub was going to get something enduring. She wanted something like that. But she also wanted him. She brushed away a moth wing of fear. Not now. Not in these precious moments with him.

"This doesn't look like it's going to end any time soon," he remarked as he sipped his beverage.

"Would you be appalled if I told you I was in no hurry?"

He glanced over his shoulder, smiling. "I wouldn't. Unfortunately, it might be better for my herd if the wind died down some. I wish Winona had indicated how long this was supposed to last."

"Believing her now?"

He turned from the window, and his expression had grown serious. "Don't you? This wasn't in the weather forecast. Not even a hint of it. How the hell did she know?"

Jenn looked down, uneasiness creeping into her. "I don't know."

"Me either." He turned back to the window. "Maybe you should talk to her."

"Why?" Jenn felt herself stiffening, all relaxation leaving the day. "To hear some useless psychic claptrap?"

He faced her. "I don't know that's why she wants to talk to you. She's been around for a while, that woman.

And not just here. Maybe she learned something about you."

"Nobody else seems to know a damn thing about me."

"Nobody else is Winona. She's been around these parts longer than most, and she hears a lot that folks don't tell anyone else. She might have heard something. Hell, for all I know, she recognized you."

"Then why didn't she just come out and say so?"

He shrugged one shoulder. "Would you want her telling anyone except you? And you're avoiding her."

She looked down, blindly staring at the blanket snugly wrapped over her breasts, at the mug she cradled in both hands. He was right, but that only made her stomach sink more.

"I get the problem," he said. "You want to know and you don't want to know. You're afraid of both. The question is which scares you more?"

"I came all the way out here looking," she said quietly, as her nerve endings began to jitter with anxiety.

"I know. Then you kind of stopped dead in the water, didn't you? How hard have you looked since you got here? Are you just waiting for the decision to be taken out of your hands?"

That was a fair question. Was that what she was doing, just waiting for answers to drop into her lap? Certainly, finding friends here had made the empty spaces in her memory somewhat easier to tolerate, uncomfortable though she often was with her own evasions and her inability to fit. Was she moving on in some way or dead in the water, as he suggested? Certainly, the compulsion that had carried her to this town seemed to have changed in the months she had been here.

Her psychologist had advised her to make the present her life, and not pursue her past, a past that might or might not return to her. If anyone was proof of the old saw that the only moment you really had was the instant in your grasp, she was it. Had she been making peace of a sort with that? Or had her compulsion waned out of fear that she had come close to her answers?

All of a sudden, Braden squatted in front of her. He took the mug from her and placed it on the table then grasped her hands. "It's your decision," he said quietly. "I'm sorry if I upset you. I'm just trying to understand."

"If I can't understand, how can you? Damn, Braden, I was driven, I couldn't give up the looking, the searching. The need for answers. Now…I don't know. It's like I got halfway and then stopped."

"Maybe because you don't know how to move forward now? You found a place that fits what you were looking for. Like you said, it's probably not the exact place, but it's a close enough fit. If you don't want to know any more than you do right now, that's okay. I'm not trying to push you. I'm certainly not the one with the need to know your past. I kinda like the woman in front of me right now."

God, she liked this man. With just a few words, he could warm her emotional soul. Freeing her hand, she reached out to cup his cheek, feeling the day's growth of beard stubble, reveling in his warmth and his very solid reality. "So it wouldn't bother you not to know anything else about me?"

Her heart nearly stopped as he said, "Oh, there's a lot more I want to know about you." But he was smiling, and as he continued, her moment of fear faded. "Lots more, but all about you now. If you never find out what came before you were hurt, that doesn't bother me. I'm only concerned about it bothering you."

Maybe, she thought, it was time to step out. To just admit to her friends the secret she had been keeping.

Maybe it wasn't so awful after all. It wasn't as if she had walked into some place and told them to erase her memory. "You're sure?"

"Life deals and then we deal. What more is there?"

Good question. She dropped her hand, and he clasped it once more. Closing her eyes, she leaned her head back. "Okay," she said, a decision made before she even knew it.

"Okay what?"

"I'll talk to Winona. But you better be with me because that woman makes me nervous."

"I'll be there if you want," he said. Then he chuckled. "I never thought of Winona Cobbs as a fearsome woman before."

At that, she opened her eyes and found him grinning. In spite of her anxiety over agreeing to meet the psychic, she couldn't help smiling back at him. "Well, she is."

He dropped down so that he was sitting cross-legged in front of her. "What exactly about her scares you? Did she say or do something?"

"She's never talked to me directly. It sounds crazy, but when our eyes meet, I feel something like an electric shock."

"Hmm." He dropped his gaze briefly. "I wonder if you used to know her."

She had barely considered the possibility. The one time it had occurred to her, she'd skipped away from it. Her fingers tightened around his as her heart skipped. She had to draw a deep breath, then exhale slowly to ease the sudden tension that filled her. "I don't know. It's possible, I guess."

He fell silent, clearly lost in thought, and she let him be. It was a nice picture anyway, the man who had just loved her, so handsome and appealing, framed against the flames in the stove behind him. She wished she could paint it, or that she had a camera to capture the moment.

He sighed quietly, the sound almost lost in the racket from the wind and the muffled crackle of the fire. "I'm trying to imagine what it would be like to forget my past. How it would feel not to remember all the things I do. It seems like memory is so much a part of me."

"It is," she admitted. "I miss it, though I don't know what I'm missing. But we talked about memory during my recovery, and I guess no memory is really reliable. We rewrite them all the time. That's why two people can recall the same incident and describe what happened so differently."

He looked at her. "So in a way, we're all amnesiacs."

That startled a laugh out of her. "Well…I guess you could look at it that way. How do you know your memories are accurate? I bet you rely a lot on external things, like old scars and other reminders. And continuity. Continuity is so important."

"And yours was interrupted."

"Totally. So I don't even know if the occasional thing I seem to remember is real in any sense of the word. Like telling you my name is really Jennifer. It feels right. But nobody else calls me that, so how can I be sure? You know your name is real because that's what everyone calls you."

He nodded, clearly thinking again. "A rose by any name…" Then he leaned back, propping himself on his hands. "I can't imagine it. What I *do* see is a woman who's more afraid than she should be. I watch those moments come over you, where you seem to pull inside yourself and hide. I hear the evasions."

Jenn flushed. "I'm sorry."

"I'm not. That's what first grabbed me, even more than

your beauty. It's what moved you from being a lovely wildflower by the roadside to one I wanted to pluck."

Her flush deepened. "That's awfully poetic."

He shrugged. "It's true. I saw a beautiful puzzle I wanted to solve. Well, it may never be solved, and surprisingly enough I'm okay with that. Now I don't give two figs for satisfying my own curiosity. What I want more than anything is to see you comfortable with yourself. Happy. You're so young, Jenn. The notion that this might continue to shadow your life, every word you speak, every thought you have, is damn near heartbreaking."

She had no idea how to respond to him. If he found her heartbreaking, surely he'd want to be done with her. How depressing it would be to be forever looking at someone who lived with a dark shadow and might always be unhappy because of it.

I'm learning," she said, sounding way too defensive. "I'm learning to live with it."

"I see that. Maybe I shouldn't have pressed you to talk with Winona. Hell, it just never crossed my mind that you might be making some kind of peace with yourself. You kept talking about why you'd come here, what you were seeking, and I should have considered that the reason you seemed to be holding back was because you were reaching a place where it doesn't matter as much as it did before."

"I didn't say that." Her tone took on an edge. "I know it's impossible to deal with this mess. *You* don't have to."

His face darkened. "I'm almost positive that's not what I was trying to say. Do you want me to try again, or do you just want to have a fight?"

Her hands had tightened into fists, and urges warred in her. She didn't really want him poking around inside her, yet she didn't want him to stop. God, she was getting sick of her own internal struggles to go one way or the other on anything. Yes, no, she had turned into one big flip-flopper.

She squeezed words out past a throat every bit as tight as her hands. "Try again."

"I'm working my way toward understanding. I'm not the most tactful of guys. Hell, I spend my life with animals and cowboys, not exactly good practice for dealing with sensitive things. I like to bull my way through, knock over barriers rather than go around them. So all I was saying was, I guess I didn't think this through all the way. Not unusual. And all I meant was, I'm sorry if I've been pushing you in ways you don't like. No promises that I won't do it again."

He sat up. "In fact, if you change your mind about seeing Winona, I won't argue. How the hell would I know for sure if it would help? I like to solve problems, yes, but this is *your* problem, and you get to decide how it's done. That's all I was trying to get at. As for me not having to deal with it, well, it's kinda late for that. I care and want to help. Don't ever think I don't. But that doesn't mean I'm not that old bull in the china shop."

Her hands had knotted tightly around a fold in the blanket, but as she listened to him, they loosened. She couldn't doubt his sincerity and let go of the flare of anger. This poor guy. He was trying to be careful and nice, the situation *was* impossible, from the inside or out, and she needed to share it with him. She couldn't do that if she pushed him away.

"I'm sorry, Braden," she offered.

"No need to be sorry. I'll put my foot in it again. All I ask is that you let me know when I do."

"Fair enough." She watched as he rose to his feet and

walked over to the window. Nightfall was coming early, even for here.

Why, she wondered, *did* she feel compelled to share this with him? She was only just getting to know him. One of her girlfriends would have been the more obvious choice. But she guessed she had been afraid of her own attraction for him, and didn't want to risk getting any closer if he might run when he learned the truth.

He hadn't run. He was trying to understand the incomprehensible, and in his own way to help her with it. Like asking her to speak to Winona. She still wasn't sure she'd do that, but his suggestion had been meant to be helpful. Like he said, he wanted to solve problems. Unfortunately, she couldn't be solved.

Struggling free of the blanket, she stood and wrapped it around her, going to stand beside him at the window.

He reached out an arm and drew her close to his side without a word. That simple welcome made her eyes prickle with tears. God, how she needed that. Welcome. Warmth. Caring without secrets. He quieted everything inside her, and she was content to just lean against him and soak it up.

It was a dangerous feeling, that she was at home in Braden's arms, but she couldn't argue with it. Instead, she savored the peace he gave her.

Braden was glad that she trusted him enough to come stand with him and let him embrace her. He felt as if they'd traveled a lot of hard ground today together. Their lovemaking had been like fireworks on the Fourth of July, an interlude of awesomeness and pleasure, but so far just an interlude.

This woman had serious problems, problems he couldn't really help her with. He hadn't been kidding when he said he liked her just as she was, and it didn't matter to him whether she ever had a past, but he knew it mattered to her.

He hated the helpless feeling. He'd never liked being helpless, always wanted to do something, a character facet that had gotten him into trouble at times. Maybe it was getting him into trouble again, this time on totally unknown territory. What the hell did he really know about what this might be like for her?

She could speak the words, try to explain, but he couldn't get inside her head and experience it. He could never really know.

That was true with everyone. He wasn't a fool. All you ever got to know was what they showed on the outside, what they told you. You could try to imagine walking in their shoes, but in a case like this, imagination fell way short. He had no comparison at all.

He just knew he liked her, wanted her, and wanted to help however he could. Wounded birds had led him down a path to trouble before. It was the main reason he didn't date much anymore.

But here he was again. A smart man would bail. Not him. He might be as stupid as all get out, but he knew Jenn elicited something in him no other woman had. Couldn't put his finger on it, but it was more than wanting her and wanting to help. Standing with her like this, holding her, he felt a quiet inside. A good quiet. Like everything was right for once.

So okay, they'd deal. *He'd* deal.

"Braden?"

A long time must have passed. It was damn near pitch-black outside, and all he could see was the snow near the window, catching the firelight from inside and blowing around like a million sparkling embers. "Hmm?"

"That bull in the china shop?"

"What about it?"

"I saw a TV show where the hosts actually put a couple of bulls in a china shop setup. They didn't bump a thing."

Was she trying to tell him something? He twisted to look at her, and he saw a small, quiet smile on her lips. "Yeah?" he asked.

"Yeah."

His spirits lifted. Everything was okay. "You asked for it now."

"What did I ask for?" She looked a bit confused.

"Me. You. Lady, I'm about to ravage you again."

"If that was ravaging earlier, I'll take a double helping."

Then she laughed, and the sound filled his heart with gladness. For a bull in a china shop, he clearly hadn't managed to break anything. Yet.

He made their nest of blankets once again in front of the fire. "Is this soft enough for you?"

"Like I'd even notice?" Wrapped in her blanket, she stood watching him with a passion-softened smile that made his heartbeat quicken. Then she dropped the blanket, revealing her full glory, and stepped into the middle of the pallet. Offering herself.

He stripped as fast as he could then paused to caress her with his gaze. "You are exquisite," he murmured. Every line, every curve of her, called to him. Her breasts, just right as far as he was concerned, nipples already puckering in their ring of pink areolas, and not from the cold. It was warm in here now, very warm. Perfect for being naked together.

Her hips flared, not a boy's but a woman's, begging

for a man's hands to grip them. The tight thatch of golden curls between her thighs covered secrets he wanted to explore in more ways than one.

Down her legs, nicely shaped, to delicate ankles and small feet with high arches. A woman built to be the stuff of a man's dreams for years to come.

The stuff of his dreams.

Then he saw that she was eyeing him in the same way. Realizing it ratcheted his hunger up even higher. But instead of acting, he forced himself to hold still. Except that he spread his arms a bit.

"Help yourself," he said. He wasn't surprised that the words sounded thick. He'd been almost unable to push them out. The air in the room began to perfume with their own musky scents, a heady brew.

She took him at his word, shyly at first then more boldly. Stepping toward him, she placed her hands on his shoulders, tracing the muscles hard work had built into him, following the lines of his arms to his hands, then sweeping back up to trace over his chest. She learned something when she brushed over his small, hardened nipples, and he saw the knowledge appear on her face.

Leaning in, she drew one into her mouth and sucked it the way he had done to her. Throwing back his head, he pulled in as much air as he could, wondering if he could hang on to his self-control much longer, telling himself he must. But passion pounded in him, reaching to the farthest corners of his being.

Then she released him. He had to fight an urge to pull her back, in order to let her continue her exploration.

She walked around behind him and ran her palms over his shoulders and back. "You have a lot of scars," she murmured. "Barbed wire?"

"Mostly. Other things, too, nothing very serious."

"What's serious?"

"Anything that can't be patched with some gauze and tape. I've only needed stitches a few times." And talking was all but impossible. How could she want to talk?

Her hands wandered down to the hard hills of his rump. He drew a ragged breath and forced himself to hold still even as his entire body tightened with an urge to pounce.

"Buns of steel," she said, her voice holding a teasing note.

How could she want to tease right now? He could barely breathe and hold still. "Saddle," he said shortly.

"Long, long hours," she surmised.

Oh man, just let him hang on a little longer.

Then she came back round to his front. "Am I torturing you?"

Considering she looked like a cat that was enjoying a bowl of cream, he supposed she wanted to think so. That kind of tickled him through the haze of desire that verged on blinding him.

"And this," she said.

She might as well have hit him with an arc welder as her hand closed around his erection.

"Mmm," she whispered as she stroked him. "I like this…"

That did it. Galvanized, he grabbed her and carried her down to the blankets. His turn now.

He made her pay. With mouth, tongue and hands, he traced her all over, tormenting her breasts with licks, sucks and nips until she cried out, and her nails dug into him. A despairing cry escaped her when he pulled back for a moment, but only a moment. Then downward he moved, across her smooth belly, causing ripples of excitement to pass through the muscles there. He could feel them, could feel the way her hips had begun small helpless movements.

With his hands he pushed her legs wide open and upward. Her eyes fluttered, widening briefly, then closing as she accepted her vulnerability.

He dove then, bringing his face down to that thatch of curls, parting her, using his tongue to lash that most sensitive nub of nerves until her restless pitching and moaning told him she was past ready. Still he kept on, plunging his tongue into her as he meant to plunge himself soon. Shudders ran through her; she bucked.

But he wasn't done. Back to that silky, swollen knot of nerves, using his tongue, he drove her onward until she was helpless to the needs, helpless in her drive for completion. Finally, she crested, with a keening so tight and thin he could feel the moment himself.

Only then did he settle himself between her legs and plunge into her. He had another secret to show her about her womanhood.

Jenn didn't think she'd ever move again. Three orgasms. *Three*! She'd heard about it, but had never believed she would know what it was like. But Braden had just shown her, carrying her to the top and over repeatedly.

She was exhausted, amazed and filled with stars of a new kind. Weakened, she lay in his arms, totally unaware of everything but her own wonder and Braden. Everything else that had preoccupied her for so long faded into the background as she emerged into the discovery of a whole new world.

Finally, she had to move, however weakly. He surprised her by lifting her until she rested on top of him, bathed in the warmth from the fire. Her head collapsed

onto his shoulder, and her face tucked into his neck. He
smelled so good!

"Wow," she whispered.

"Wow," he agreed, his voice rusty.

He reached up to stroke her hair, to run his palm over
her back and bottom, gentle caresses. This time they
brought her no fire, just the quietude he had given her
earlier. Peace, such a stranger to her, found her in his
arms.

For the first time, building a future without her past
actually seemed possible. Her therapist had suggested
she try it, and if her future could be full of memories like
this, who needed a past? Whatever she might remember
would pale to insignificance beside this.

Of course, there was no guarantee there would be
any more of this, either. No promises had been made,
nor could they make them at this point. It was entirely
possible that he would walk out of here after the storm
passed and there would be nothing more between them
except friendship.

Could she deal with that? She supposed she could.
She'd dealt with worse, like being alone and rootless in a
strange world. He had showed her life could still be wonderful anyway, and that she could conceivably find happi-
ness despite everything. Maybe the answers didn't lie in
what she'd forgotten, but in the person she became now.

She stirred a little, wondering at the direction of her
thoughts. It seemed like such a seismic shift after her
obsession with her past. Maybe it wasn't to be trusted.
Maybe when Braden walked out of here, she'd find herself back on the same hamster wheel, with an added wrin-
kle: longing for something she could never have. Because
she doubted she would be the woman who put an end to
Braden's bachelorhood. She didn't feel as if she could

possibly measure up to all he must want. Given that at thirty-four he still hadn't married, or from what she gathered even had a long-term relationship, there was no reason to think she might be the one he was looking for. If he was even looking.

Crazy thoughts, she told herself. Looking so far ahead along a road that was as blank as most of the way behind her…just an exercise in wishful, foolish thinking. The only moment she could truly claim was the present one.

Drawing a deep breath, yanking her mind back from the chasm of the future as well as the chasm of the past, she returned to the now. Lying in Braden's arms. Being held and caressed by him. This was the purest magic, and she needed to focus on it. On him. On whatever time he chose to give her.

Tomorrow would take care of itself. Somehow, through all her travails, it had always managed to do so.

A thought struck her. At once she stiffened, rolled off him and sat up.

"Jenn? What's wrong?"

She drew up her knees, wrapping her arms around them, and turned to look at him. "Nothing. I just had a thought."

He sat up halfway, propping himself on his elbow. "Which was?"

"That I don't know any more about tomorrow than I know about my past. Sure, I imagine it's there. I imagine I'll see you. I imagine that if the storm's gone, I'll get back to town. Or see my friends, or talk to them on the phone."

He nodded encouragingly.

"But I don't know that. I fill my picture of tomorrow with imagination because I can't really know. I guess…" She hesitated, trying to find the words. "The future is only as real as I imagine it. I could say the same about the past. Both are only as real as I make them in my head. Maybe I'm obsessing too much about my lost memories. Yeah, I'd like to know who I was, but if I never remember…well, maybe it's an uncertainty the same as the ones I could have about the future."

Now he sat up the rest of the way. A few minutes passed and she waited, though for what, she didn't know. His approval? His disagreement?

"You know," he said finally, "that's a pretty heavy thought."

"Silly?"

He shook his head. "Not at all. It drew me up short, thinking about it that way. It's kind of like what you said about continuity. That's the only thing that really gives us a sense of our place."

She nodded. "Exactly. We assume there's this unbroken flow, but mine got interrupted, like you said. I don't know who I used to be. But I could just as easily say I don't know who I'll be tomorrow. Change is constant."

"Think that'll work for you?" He cocked a brow at her.

"I don't know," she admitted. "It's just a thought. Right now I feel so good, I don't care about any of it. I could feel differently again tomorrow."

Yes, she could, he thought as they dressed. The stove was still making heat, but something had come into the cabin with them. Maybe it was the shadow of her past, or the difficulties that still lay ahead of her as she tried to find some peace within herself. Whatever, the interlude was over for now. Reality had firmly stepped back into the room.

Although, what they had just shared was reality. He hoped she understood that. Beautiful, exquisite, mind-blowing reality. Not everything real had to be bad. He wondered if she could even understand that anymore, given her long search for self and place. Maybe for her, life could be seen only as a struggle, one full of unmet needs and a whole lot of fear.

That notion disturbed him deeply. He'd led a mostly blessed life, and he knew it. Family, friends, work that he loved. The little clouds that had visited his life had been minimized by all those he cared about.

She didn't have that support network. She'd been left alone with a private, raging storm, one every bit as bad as the blizzard outside.

They sat at the small table again, as if she wanted some distance. Their lovemaking still perfumed the air, but it was fading. Maybe she needed it to. He simply didn't know how to figure her yet.

"I'm sorry," she said a little later. "I feel like I just crashed a party and sent everyone running."

He shook his head a little. "You didn't crash anything. You didn't ruin anything. We can bring the magic back later if you want."

"So you're not mad at me? I feel utterly self-centered."

"I'm not mad. Not even a little. Just wish I could help more. And I don't think you're self-centered. You've been wrestling all alone with a big problem for a long time. It's not the kind of problem anyone could just forget for long. And I think you've got a lot of stuff inside you probably need to share, especially considering you haven't even told your friends about this. I'm willing to listen. I don't mind at all. I'm still wrapping my brain around all of this, but like I said, no amount of wrapping is going to let me know what this is like for you."

"I wish, I truly wish, I could just give all this up, just forget, just move on."

"I'm sure you do, but this is a little bigger than most things. It's right up at the top of big things, in fact. Harder to just put behind us. I actually think you're doing pretty well for someone who's had such a major trauma."

"I wouldn't know." She drummed her fingers briefly. "See, that's the other thing. I don't know what I know. I remember how to cook, obviously. I can still speak and understand. I never forgot how to drive, how to dress, any of that stuff. But I lack comparisons for a lot of things, because I don't have a memory of where I've been and what I've done. Sometimes I'll make a judgment about something and then wonder if I'm right because I don't have a storehouse of memories against which to measure it."

"Such as?" He was genuinely interested in this part. Jenn was such a fascinating, beautiful puzzle.

"Like what you just said. I know total amnesia is rare because they told me so. I also know I had a trauma because of the scar on my head. Whether I'm dealing with it well or not… How would I know?"

"Not many of us would have an answer to that, I'm afraid."

It pleased him to see her relax into a smile. "True that," she said.

But he understood what she was trying to say. "Do you spend a lot of time questioning yourself?"

"At the beginning I did a whole lot more of it. I questioned pretty much everything I did, so maybe it was good that I felt so driven to find my place, if not myself. It gave me a purpose. Otherwise, I might have dithered myself to death. But now…not so much. I can accept that at some level I knew coming to Rust Creek Falls was a good decision. That I feel it's close to whatever I needed, and I don't question the fact that I don't feel like I came from here. I'm learning to trust myself more, I guess."

"That's a good thing."

Even in the dim firelight, he thought she looked embarrassed.

"Evasion," she said, "has become almost natural. I don't think I'm lying, but how would I know? If I don't have an answer, I try to find a truthful way not to answer. But you noticed that, didn't you?"

"It was one of the things that first got my attention. I thought you were beautiful the few times I'd seen you around, but that night at my parents' house, you seemed to slip away like a stream rushing downhill."

"You have a nice way of describing things. Also a nonjudgmental one."

He couldn't resist. "How would you know?"

Her eyes widened, and for an instant he thought she would blow up at him, then she got it and laughed. "Good one, Braden. Well, that's my reaction, and I'm sticking to it."

He had no doubt she was a spirited, determined woman, but it was nice to see her drop her guard enough to let it show. "You're safe with me," he blurted, then wondered if he had just promised more than he should have. He knew nothing about her beyond what she had shared. There was always the possibility that she might turn out to have once been a very different woman. Well, he'd cross that river if they came to it.

Because as the evening deepened, and the storm continued to batter the world, he felt tendrils growing between them. Links, ties, bindings. She was melding herself with him in a way that ought to heighten his caution, especially under these circumstances.

But he liked what was happening between them. Liked getting to know her, liked seeing her face across the table, liked the way they had made love together. Despite the risks, he didn't want to damage even a single tender shoot of the intimacy they were beginning to share—the real intimacy of her problems, her fears, her efforts to deal with them. For the first time, he wished he was more than just a cowboy. Someone with the training to really help her somehow. What, a private detective?

He almost laughed at himself. If the cops hadn't been able to figure out who she was, what made him think he'd do any better? All he had to offer was Winona's insistence on talking to her, a pretty slim lead. Maybe the woman had heard something. Maybe she had recognized Jennifer somehow. But as it stood, he didn't know what the psychic had to offer, and in a way he felt bad for pressing Jenn to see her when Winona clearly made her so uncomfortable.

But, he thought, maybe there was a reason for that. Maybe Winona was connected in some way with Jenn's past. Maybe at some level, Jenn recognized her.

Which made her desire to avoid Winona even more interesting. Assuming that was the case, of course. She wanted to know but didn't want to know. She'd said as much herself. She feared not liking what she might learn, which was perfectly understandable, but she also couldn't live with not knowing.

A hell of a dilemma.

"Okay," he said, "a man's gotta eat. Eggs aren't going to carry me through. Hungry?"

She seemed glad to change the subject. This time he didn't make the decision, but invited her to look through the supplies he'd brought and whatever remained in her fridge that looked good while he put some more wood on the fire. He'd made the last pot of coffee with snow because when the power went out it had taken her well pump with it, so he hunted up the biggest pot he could find and went to get some more snow to boil on the stove.

"You need a bigger pot," he remarked as he prepared to step outside with one of her saucepans.

She laughed, and the sound followed him until it faded into the winter squall as he closed the door. The move outside was bracing, moving him from a warm, snuggly cocoon into the harsher world of nature's rage.

He gave himself a lecture on common sense, caution, not moving too fast, watching his step...and then forgot it all when he went back inside.

The cabin had transformed. She had lit a few candles, bringing light to the darker places, and her smile was brighter than all of them combined. He didn't want to be anywhere else in the world.

And he didn't care how dangerous this might be.

Chapter Nine

Morning brought a brilliant, snow-covered world. Sometime during the night, the wind had died and the storm had passed. By noon the plow managed to find its way to Jenn's cabin, and Braden departed after a few lingering kisses. He had to check on the herd, had to know how much damage they'd suffered.

Jenn understood, but ached as she watched him drive away. He'd said he would call, but there was still no cell phone reception, and the power hadn't yet been restored.

Before leaving, Braden had dug her car out of the snowdrift that had buried it. She wondered if it would even start, but a strange sort of ennui seemed to fill her. She thought of going to town to check on her friends, then assumed they were probably better off than she was.

She had reached some kind of cusp, she realized. Caught between past and present, trying to cling to the idyll she had shared with Braden, reluctant to go out into the world and shatter it.

She had decisions to make. Friends to see. It might be easier to get by in town. She had no doubt that Vanessa, Mallory, Cecelia or one of the others would offer her a sofa if she needed a warm place to stay.

But Braden had left her with the supplies and a truckload of wood right outside her door. She had no *need* to go anywhere. Not right now.

Things inside her seemed to have rearranged, and she spent the afternoon sitting in front of the fire, trying to sort through them.

Pursuing her past could end right here and now, she realized. Braden had opened up possibilities that overwhelmed her. Maybe he would be part of her future, maybe he wouldn't, but he had certainly taught her that there *could* be a future.

As for her past, what did she want from it? The sorry fact was, even if she had the details, such as where she had come from, what her real name was, who her parents had been, they would mean little to her in any real sense. Without her memory of all that, she would probably feel no real connection at all.

But even those bare facts could still anchor her. Answers to the simplest questions eluded her, such as exactly how old she was, when her birthday was, where she had been born. She supposed there were people in the world without amnesia who couldn't accurately answer those questions, too, but in this country, everybody she met had an answer.

Well, searching or not, she had to start making firm moves toward a future. She couldn't continue to live as if she were going to pack up and move at any moment. She needed work, she needed to plan, she needed to settle.

She needed to accept the way things were.

Easier said than done, of course. The desire to fill in the blanks had been driving her almost since the beginning, when it became clear she wouldn't have a spontaneous recovery. It had given her the purpose that had been riven from her by amnesia.

Maybe it was time to find a new purpose, if she could. Searching hadn't done a whole lot for her. She'd remembered her name, or at least the name that felt right, spontaneously. She'd recognized that mountain, but it was utterly without context. She'd come to a town that she knew instinctively wasn't her home, but it felt close to home.

All that effort for a few little tidbits, none of which really anchored her, especially since she didn't know if any of it was real. The name Jennifer had popped out of her; it had felt right. But for all she knew, it was the name of a character from a movie or book that she liked.

If someone walked up to her and handed her her birth certificate, she wasn't sure she would feel any more rooted. Not without the all-important memories.

She had to push her search for answers onto the back burner and get on with life. Otherwise, she'd end up as crazy as Homer Gilmore, wandering the world and muttering strange words that nobody could understand.

He was another one that made her nervous, she was sorry to admit. She cared that he was homeless, but his rambling kept her at a distance. Maybe because she somehow recognized that she wasn't so very different from him. She had a roof now. With the coins around her neck, she would probably always have a roof, but otherwise? Otherwise, she'd become a daft old lady on an endless quest.

Winona and Homer. Two people she avoided like the plague. Now she wondered why.

Damn, she was getting a headache. She'd boiled some snow earlier for drinking water, and went to take a couple of ibuprofen. Maybe she needed another pot of coffee.

But she nixed that idea as soon as she realized she was pacing her tiny cabin, rubbing her arms, and fighting a deep-rooted anxiety again.

Think about Braden, she told herself. Think about the hours they'd spent making love. She had been very much in the present then, and now she had a past to remember: those hours with Braden. A past *worth* remembering.

She wanted more memories like that.

"Slacker." That was the first word out of Dallas's mouth when Braden got back to the ranch. His brother, bundled up like the Abominable Snowman, was carrying a calf into the barn, its mooing mother right at his heels.

Braden didn't answer directly. "How bad?"

"Not that bad," Dallas admitted. "We've got most of the calves who seem to be suffering from the cold in the barn. The herd did pretty well with the rest. We're okay, bro, just need to help these few along."

"So no losses?"

"Not yet. You should ride out and check some more. I'm not sure we got them all. So how's your new lady?"

Braden wanted to ignore that question. He didn't want his brothers trampling all over his time with Jenn in their usual teasing way. He wanted to protect those hours, and her, from their raucous commentary. And that was about as likely to happen as waving his arm to make all the snow vanish. "Any place you haven't checked yet?"

"Snow's deep in places. We could have missed some out there. So it's like that?"

"What?" Braden tensed, ready for the inevitable jibe.

But Dallas surprised him as he set the calf on its weak legs next to the mother. It began to suckle almost immediately. Compared to the outside world, the barn was warm and cozy. Then his gaze settled on Braden. "Just wondered if I'd ever see you so taken."

Braden didn't even know how to reply to that. Was he taken? More than he ever had been before. He felt as if he was carrying something special inside him, something he didn't want to have sullied by anything. Without replying, he simply went to saddle his horse. Livestock first. Always first. Then everything else. He hoped Jenn could understand that, because if she couldn't, it wouldn't matter how taken he was with her. She just simply wouldn't fit into his world.

The afternoon stretched into long, cold hours until waning light forced him to head back. As far as he could tell, they'd skipped their way through this blizzard with no real loss. Amazing. Despite his confident comments to Jenn yesterday morning, he'd been worried. The older cattle could pretty much find their windbreaks and keep moving enough to share their heat. The calves had less endurance, and he'd feared some losses, if not big ones.

But somehow their luck had held. He found no more troubled calves, nor any sign of dead ones. A storm like this in the spring, right after calving, often had a different ending. Or an early-season storm in October.

Which was not to say the herd was looking happy. Some of those bovine eyes seemed to regard him with reproach, as if he were responsible for this messy weather. Overhead, the cloud cover continued to break up, showing patches of dark blue as the day waned. They sure needed a few sunny days now.

Back at the barn, he helped throw hay to the sequestered cows, and check the calves for any sign of frostbite. So far so good, but the barn was filled to the rafters now. He hoped they'd have less to do by morning.

They couldn't shovel fast enough, he thought with mild amusement.

He heard the dinner bell clanging from the main house, but instead of joining his brother on the trek to a huge, warm dinner, he tried his cell phone again. On the ranch they used satellite phones so they wouldn't have trouble keeping in touch, but Jenn was on a cell phone, and he hoped the towers were functioning again. He needed to hear the sound of her voice.

When she answered, he felt as if warmth poured into his heart through his ear. "How's it going?" he asked her. "I can tell you got your phone back, but what about your power?"

"Not yet. But I'm positively becoming a pioneer woman. I've got a good fire going, and I was about to cook over it. See what you've done to me?"

He laughed. "I wish I could get over there."

"How's the ranch? Your herd?"

He was touched that she even asked. He'd dated a few women who wouldn't have given a damn, and a few who'd only pretended to. It hadn't taken him long to decide they weren't cut out to be part of his life. Everything revolved around this ranch.

"We're fine. We have a barn full of chilled calves and their mamas, but we didn't lose a one."

"That's great news!"

"I think so. Especially since I bailed out yesterday."

She fell silent for a moment, and he could hear noise on the line. Then she said, "You didn't have to come to my rescue, Braden. I'm not saying I didn't appreciate it, but considering how important those animals are...well..."

"Stop," he said. "There wasn't a whole lot I could do anyway until the storm finished. All I lost was a few hours, and my brother took care of it. Another time I might have to make a different decision, but I'm glad I made the one I did."

"I'm glad you did, too," she said, her voice seeming to hold secret promises, and warming him even more.

"Did you get into town today?"

"No," she admitted. "I wasted the whole afternoon. And Mallory's on call-waiting right now. I suppose she wonders if I'm still alive. The phone just started working again."

"You go talk to her. If I can, I'll try to come over after dinner. If that's okay?"

"It's always okay."

He hoped she meant that. Suddenly very happy, he whistled as he walked up to the house. He was sure he was in for the teasing that Dallas had avoided, but surprisingly he didn't care anymore.

Jenn spent a while on the phone with Mallory and Lily, who wanted to add her own two cents. She, it seemed, quite liked Jenn's new nickname and wanted her to know it. Mallory didn't ask any questions about it, which was really tactful of her, but talked instead about how she, Lily and Caleb had spent the whole day shoveling snow. "Damn, it built up between the buildings. Some of our older neighbors really needed help. Is your cabin buried?"

"Along one side, but it's not in the way. No complaints here."

They chatted for a few more minutes, then got off the phone to take care of their own matters.

Her dinner was interrupted by calls from Vanessa and a couple of others from the Newcomers Club, and by the time the calls stopped coming, she realized that Rust Creek Falls was trying to make her feel at home. Only her own resistance stood in the way.

Then Cecelia called just as she started to boil water in which to take a stab at washing dishes.

"Hey," Cecelia said. "You're still alive."

"That's the rumor."

Cecelia laughed. "Got your power back? We have it, but I hear it's still a little spotty."

"I'm probably at the bottom of the list, out here."

"But you're okay? Do you need anything?"

"If I did, I'd come to town. I'm learning how to take full advantage of a woodstove."

"I thought that thing terrified you."

"It used to," Jenn admitted, without telling Cecelia how the change had come about. "We do what we must and all that. So what's happening? You all are okay, right?"

"We're fine. We were prepared, thanks to Winona."

That woman again. Jenn's hand tightened on her phone, and she feared she might disconnect by accident. Finger by finger she eased her grip and tried to answer lightly. "I guess I should have listened. But really, I'm okay. I have everything I need."

"You can get out of there, can't you?"

"All shoveled and plowed out."

That was when she heard Cecelia hesitate. "Julie? I mean Jenn. Damn, I *will* get used to this."

"I'll answer to either," Jenn assured her.

"It's not that. It's…well, I had to run to the grocery today because while we got ready in every other way, I forgot birdseed."

"Birdseed?" Jenn practically gaped into the phone.

"Hey listen, I've got a hundred sparrows dependent on the feeder Nick gave me as an early present. If you had to look at them all fluffed up out there, huddling on windowsills to stay warm, knowing that feeder was empty, you'd run to the store, too."

"Someday I need to see this. Okay, you're right. If I had a hundred birds looking all pathetic here, I'd have run to the store, too."

Cecelia laughed, but it didn't sound quite natural. Jenn had had enough. "Cecelia, what's wrong?"

Cecelia's sigh was audible. "Nothing really. It's more like weird."

"So spill."

"When I was at the store, I ran into Winona Cobbs." Tension filled Jenn all over again. "And?"

"Look, I know you don't like her. Not everyone does. There are plenty who think she's a crackpot to be avoided. But anyway..."

Jenn waited impatiently, wanting this conversation to come to a conclusion, feeling like she was on tenterhooks. "What?"

"She said she wanted to talk to you. I was to tell you that. Then she said something that was really weird. She said Homer knows. Now what in the hell would Homer know? Wandering around talking about babies lost and found, the past being present and all that stuff. I'm surprised the guy remembered to come out of the storm."

"You're disturbed because she said something about Homer?"

"No," Cecelia answered. "I'm disturbed because...well, only a couple of us know you decided you wanted to be called by your old nickname. Not a problem, but not exactly anything anyone's gossiping about. It's only been a few weeks, and it's just not that important. Julie, Jenn, who cares, right?"

Jenn closed her eyes and leaned against the short little counter. She could hear the water bubbling on the stove now, but it seemed a long way away. "So? I don't care who knows."

"I imagine not. I just want you to know that because it'll explain why I'm so...weirded out by this. When I saw Winona, she said I was to tell *Jennifer* that she wanted to talk to her. I must have looked astonished because then she said she meant the Jennifer everyone called Julie."

* * *

For a long time after the phone call ended, Jennifer ignored the boiling water and sat staring at the fire. Winona must have heard from somewhere what had happened at the gift wrapping. Someone must have overheard.

But that didn't answer the question of why the psychic had now told two people she wanted to talk to Jenn.

She must know something. Braden was right; she might have just heard something or figured out something. It didn't have to be all spooky or weird, just casual knowledge Winona had come by in a conversation. Or something she might have remembered from the past. Simple, ordinary knowledge.

Or she might know nothing, really, might have sensed Jenn's antipathy, and wanted to make a point of some kind.

But for all Winona made her feel uneasy, Jenn didn't think the psychic was that kind of person. People might be weirded out by her, but she'd never heard anyone accuse the woman of unkindness.

All of which left her staring into the gaping maw of her past again. Did she want whatever information Winona might have? Could she believe it regardless? She was certainly a perfect victim for lies. When she thought about it, she was lucky she hadn't been scammed a dozen times over. Like her necklace. Only her good fortune had brought an honest expert to her. Someone else could have taken advantage of her to get the wealth off her neck.

Or maybe not. She fingered the coins again and knew that she didn't want to part with her only link to her past. She'd had enough trouble emotionally just selling one of them, and she'd done that only so she could get out here and...

Search for her past.

Damn, she was going to be haunted forever. Every time she made up her mind to let it go, she faced once again her utter inability to do so.

The sound of a truck engine caught her attention, and she went to the steamy window. That boiling water was turning this place into a sauna. Dang, she hoped the pot wasn't ready to boil dry.

Using her sleeve, she wiped away the steam and peered out. Braden was pulling up out front, his truck a now-familiar sight. He'd managed to come!

In an instant her heart soared. She'd been moony all day over him, remembering his every word and touch, and hoping against hope that she'd see him again soon. Her very first crush, insofar as she knew, and she was suffering all the aching, yearning pangs that evidently went with it.

Braden, Braden, Braden. His name had become a constant drumbeat in her blood. Every memory of him caused her heart to jump. The need to see him was becoming as overwhelming as her search for her past.

Smiling now, she went to open the door for him. His smile seemed to stretch from ear to ear.

"Damn," he said, kicking the door closed behind him. He swept her into a hug, pressing her against his cold outer clothes. "This day was endless. I thought I'd never get back to you."

"I couldn't wait," she admitted.

"Music to my ears." Then he kissed her, long, hard and deep. Inside she melted into a puddle of yearning, but instead of taking the kiss further, he broke it off. Disappointment speared through her.

He started stripping his outerwear. "My God, are you trying to turn this place into a sauna?"

She laughed easily enough. "Not on purpose. I was

boiling water for dishes and got distracted by phone calls."

He finished hanging his gear then brushed another kiss on her lips and headed for the stove. "Um, we need water here."

"Maybe I should just give up the project." And make love with him. For hours and hours...

But he seemed in no rush, and she began to wonder if he didn't want her again. Instead, he grabbed another saucepan from her kitchen, ducked outside just long enough to fill it with snow, then dumped the snow into the boiling pot. "How desperately do you want to wash dishes?" he asked.

"Not very," she admitted. Not now that he was here.

"I'll help. Sorry, I'm frozen. Dinner didn't even warm me up. I'm not usually such a wuss, but I spent all afternoon on horseback, and I think the cold reached my bones. I blasted the heater in my truck, and I still feel like ice."

Sympathy began to replace her disappointment. "I'll make us some coffee. You sit close to that fire."

He sat on the floor while she put the pot on the stove. "Maybe I should just stop boiling water."

"Nah," he said. "I just realized that this is the first time in hours that I could actually breathe through my nose."

"Is this unusually cold or something?"

"No." His eyes were smiling as she turned, and he reached up to tug her hand until she sat in his lap, her back cradled against his chest. "I think I didn't get enough sleep last night is all. The tank is low on energy. Now I wonder who could have been responsible for that?"

Instantly, all her worries and fears fled. He couldn't have made it any plainer that he wasn't here to tell her he was through with her. "I'm sorry."

"I most definitely am not."

She let her head fall back to rest against his shoulder. "So the cows are okay?"

"Everything is okay. I took a little ribbing, but that was inevitable. My family's not used to me being gone when there's bad weather. But what good is it to have Dallas hanging around if I have to do everything?"

She laughed again, feeling gloriously happy that he was here. The shadows that had plagued her afternoon evaporated. At least for now.

"Do you get any time off?"

"Yeah, I can take a few weeks away if I want to. Dallas could hire a hand to fill in for me. Of course, there are better times of year to do it. Calving season, for example, is one time you couldn't pry me loose from the place."

"All hands on deck?"

"Believe it. As many as we can get and hire."

"I hope I get to see it."

"If you're still here come spring, I can promise you."

If she was still here? She guessed she could understand why he might wonder. With a jolt, her thoughts came back to Winona. Her heart started hammering, and her hands tightened. She had to face this. She *had* to. She couldn't keep living with anxiety every time one woman's name came up. This was a kind of craziness on her part.

"Jenn? What's wrong? You stiffened up."

"Winona," she said through tight lips.

"What about her? Did she bother you?" He sounded ready to ride to her defense.

"No, no. It's just that Cecelia says she wants to talk to me." Then she outlined the conversation, and how weird it seemed that Winona had called her Jennifer.

Braden ran his hand down her arm. "That's strange,

all right. The only person I told you were Jenn now was Dallas, and he'd have no reason to tell anyone else."

"And I just told the girls it was my old nickname, and I wanted to go back to it. They didn't seem to care one way or another."

"Probably not." The coffee smelled done, so Jenn made herself get up to pour them some. When she returned from the kitchen area with mugs, Braden had moved to one of the chairs.

"So," he said as she poured, "what do you want to do about it?"

What she wanted was to tumble onto the floor with him, or into her bed and make love until everything else in the world vanished. She wanted to forget that anything else existed except Braden.

But she knew it wasn't going to work. No way. Winona kept popping up, and forgetting about it for a few hours wouldn't make her go away. "I'm going to have to talk to her."

Braden glanced at his watch. "I could go get her right now."

"But it's late."

"It's not that late. I know where she lives. If you want, we can just deal with this and make it stop bothering you. Man, you must feel almost stalked."

"It can wait." And yes, she was starting to feel stalked, but surely sometime tomorrow would be soon enough?

"No, it can't." He stood up and began reaching for his outerwear, showing her a determined and stubborn side she should have expected, given what he did for a living, but a side she hadn't seen before. "You need not to be worrying about this. You wanted me present when you talked to her, and given the results of this storm and all the work I have waiting for me, I can't absolutely guarantee when I'll next be able to arrange that. Will I be back tomorrow night? I hope so. But sweetie, I can't promise right now. So let's just get this problem off your plate."

"But…"

"No buts." He bent to kiss her as he started buttoning his jacket. "We're crossing this one off the list now."

She could have gone with him, but dread began to fill her so much she stayed where she was, hoping he couldn't find Winona, that she could postpone whatever this was for another day.

Facing her own cowardice never pleased her, but she was feeling like a coward now. There was so much she thought showed how tough she was, surviving the amnesia, the hunt for her past, moving across the country…then one woman reminded her of how afraid she truly was.

"Chicken," she said aloud to the empty cabin as Braden drove away. Then, mad at herself, she took the boiling water off the stove. Washing dishes could go hang.

Braden drove as fast as he dared on the slick roads. He knew he was pushing Jenn, but he was beginning to believe she needed a little pushing. It was clear to him by now that she *needed* to know something. She could talk all she wanted about moving on, but somehow everything kept coming back to her need to know her real identity.

No matter how firmly she resolved to move forward, she was far from ready to let go. And maybe Winona knew something that could help her settle it. Something that at least could give Jenn an anchor to cling to even if she never remembered. A sense of her place.

Jenn was like a leaf blowing in the wind. She needed to land somehow, and maybe all it would take were some tidbits of information. Assuming Winona really knew anything, of course, but from all he'd heard about the psychic, she didn't strike him as one to shoot her mouth off in a way that might hurt someone.

She was also as old as the hills and knew more about this area and the people in it, its history, than anyone. She'd lived in many of the towns around here, or so he'd heard. She might honestly know something. Jenn owed it to herself to find out. And he was damn sure not going to let her put off something so important when it was dangling right in front of her.

Winona answered her door on that third knock. Braden was relieved to see she was still dressed. At her age, she might have already gone to bed.

"The youngest Traub," Winona remarked. "You got through the storm."

"Yes. Ms. Cobbs…"

"Winona," the woman said sharply. Her white-as-snow hair made a wild halo around her. "It's about Jennifer. That's why you're here."

In spite of himself, Braden felt a flicker of amusement. "You don't miss much."

"I don't miss anything. When is she going to see me?"

"Right now, if you're willing."

Much to his relief, Winona was willing. She invited him in, and as she struggled to get into her winter coat and boots, he helped her as much as she would let him. Touching her reminded him of just how frail and old she was. What was he thinking, dragging her out on a cold night like this?

"About time," Winona muttered when at last she was ready to go out the door. "Been looking at that girl for months. Something about her…" She tapped her head and looked at Braden just before they stepped outside. "Too many memories. Hard to get at them all anymore."

He was too young to imagine that, but willing to take her word for it. As he helped her into the warmth of his still-running truck, he realized he was glad she had spoken of memories, not intuition. He felt a little better about what he was doing here.

If Winona actually remembered, then the dangers of giving Jenn misinformation were slim to none.

And even just a little real information might help Jenn settle. Damn, he hoped so.

But fear rode with him alongside Winona. It was entirely possible that whatever she knew could take Jenn away from here.

Like it or not, he was beginning to think he couldn't stand losing her.

Braden helped Winona over the snow and ice to Jenn's door. Lights from within told him the power had been restored. That much was good, but right now he was more worried about the reception he was going to receive after having pushed this situation on her. He hadn't listened to her objections, and he frankly wouldn't have been surprised if she slammed the door in their faces. That woman had enough tigers on her tail that he couldn't blame her for wanting to avoid him.

But everything froze as if in crystal when Jenn opened the door hesitantly. For several seconds, none of them moved. Jenn stood looking like a frightened deer as she saw Winona. Winona, however, experienced no such qualms.

"I suspected it," she said. "You're Jennifer MacCallum."

Chapter Ten

Jenn froze in shock. She hadn't expected such a blunt statement, and while the name Jennifer clearly resonated with her, MacCallum didn't.

Winona wasn't deterred. She pushed her way through the door. "Damn cold out there. A body could freeze between one breath and the next. Let an old woman in and give me some coffee if you have it."

The words galvanized Jenn. Something to do. A need to fill. She didn't know what to make of the rest, but she supposed she was now going to find out whether she wanted to or not. Braden helped Winona out of her coat, then the woman eased herself into an armchair and took the coffee from Jenn.

"Sit down, girl," she said. "I don't know what you're doing hanging around here pretending to be someone else, but you got family that hunted for you for years and are now grieving for you because they think you're dead. That's pretty sad for all of you."

Jenn didn't know how to react. She wasn't pretending anything, but she could hardly tell this woman it wasn't sad.

"Why are you calling yourself Julie Smith?"

Silence hung in the air. Jenn could barely breathe. The crackling of the fire seemed loud. She felt Braden come to stand behind her, placing his hand on her shoulder. That touch gave her strength.

Jenn gathered herself, finally reaching a decision. Braden had accepted her amnesia, and so could everyone else. She was tired of all the tiptoeing, all the evasions. Let the chips fall. "Frankly," Jenn said defiantly, "I have amnesia. I don't remember who I used to be."

"Ahh." Winona nodded, then spent a few minutes sipping coffee. As the seconds ticked by, Jenn felt as if she were being stretched on a rack. Finally, Winona spoke. "Then you need to know."

A spark of fear-fueled anger. "Maybe I don't want to know."

Winona arched a thin white eyebrow at her. "Then what are you doing here? What we want and what we need isn't always the same thing."

Too true, Jenn thought. She was caught between fear and need, virtually paralyzed except for the butterflies in her stomach with her blood hammering in fear, on the edge of fighting or fleeing.

Braden spoke. "Take it easy on her, Winona. She's had a long, hard struggle to get this far."

Winona nodded and settled back. "The girl's had a lot of hard life. Guess that hasn't changed. But good life, too, between the bad. Maybe it's time to answer all the questions and deal with all the bad, and get herself settled."

"I'm still here," Jenn said between her teeth. "Quit talking about me like I'm not."

"Part of you is here. Part of you is lost. Homer recognized you, too. Took me a while longer."

Braden spoke again. "You want to explain that?"

"Maybe I'll get to it. I got my own ways of telling a story. First off, like I said, you're Jennifer MacCallum. You have family grieving you. But no, you took a notion to run off and you never came back, and they couldn't find you. How far did you run?"

"Why do you need to know?"

"Because your folks scoured three states for you and couldn't find any trace. Finally, they got around to believing you were dead."

"For all practical purposes, I was." Jenn wished the woman would get to the point, would spare her the inquisition. Wished her heart rate would settle, and the tension seep away. She wondered if she would ever live without it again.

"Nice fire," Winona remarked. Then she drew a breath.

"Jennifer MacCallum, like I said. That's you. Born in Whitehorn."

"Whitehorn!" Braden seemed surprised.

"Where's that?" Jenn asked.

"Not all that far from here, but far enough you probably wouldn't trip into it."

"So I got close?" Jenn asked.

"You got close," he reassured her.

"Like a little homing pigeon with a glitch in the route," Winona agreed. "Guess you were trying to get home somehow."

Jenn didn't answer. She supposed she had been in her search for her past, but she still didn't feel as if she had a home, not even with a name attached to it. Whitehorn? The name didn't even ring a distant bell for her. Some of her tension was easing, however. Maybe it was Braden's hand on her shoulder, squeezing gently. Home, she realized, or as close as she could get, had become this man.

"I haven't got all night," Winona said as if they were

holding her up when she was taking her own good time about all of this. "Best get to it."

"Jennifer MacCallum." Jenn prodded her.

"That's right. Had a busy life for such a little one. Kidnapped at three…"

"Kidnapped?" Jenn stopped her. "What happened?"

"Mary Jo Kincaid ran off with you, carried you over the mountains when she took you from Whitehorn to North Dakota."

Jenn looked at Braden. "Maybe that's why I recognized the mountain."

"What mountain?" Winona asked.

"Fall Mountain," Braden answered.

Winona nodded. "That would be the one. So you recognized it?"

"It seemed familiar. But who was Mary Jo Kincaid?"

Winona rocked a little, as if she were used to sitting in a rocking chair. "You got a tangled story, Jenny. Really tangled. You want it all?"

Jenn hesitated only briefly. "Yes. All of it." Better all of it than more questions.

"Your mama ran away. Her name was Maria March. Don't know where she got off to, but your daddy was a Kincaid. Jeremiah Kincaid. The MacCallums took you as a foster child and made you their own. Must be why Mary Jo thought she should grab you from the MacCallums, you being a Kincaid and all. Jeremiah sure didn't want you much, and he was getting up there. Might as well have been a little ragamuffin except for Sterling and Jessica MacCallum. They adopted you when they got you back and brought you up."

Jenn tried to absorb this. So her birth mother hadn't wanted her, her real father hadn't been interested, and somehow she had become adopted. She was afraid to ask more about it, though, because she didn't want to distract Winona, who was at last telling her the story.

"Anyway, you grew up fine with just a few hitches. A lot of spunk, folks said. Spunk got you into trouble."

"How?"

"You ran away."

"Why? Why did I do that?"

"You got an inheritance from Jeremiah Kincaid on your twenty-first birthday. You didn't like it. You made no bones about not wanting the money because Jeremiah had been thieving it from the local Native Americans. Made himself a wealthy man that way. Now I suppose there were lots of ways you could have dealt with that. Could have given it all away, I guess. But you were hotheaded, and your parents wanted you to invest it so you'd be okay no matter what. I heard there was a big fight between you. Even told them they weren't your real parents and had no right to tell you anything."

Jennifer felt her heart sink. She had wondered if she would like the person she used to be, and right now she wasn't sure she did. Telling her adoptive parents, the people who had raised her by choice, that they weren't her real parents? She wanted to shudder. "But they did love me?"

"Enough to tear three states apart looking for you."

Jenn let that sink in, and while she couldn't recall her adoptive parents, she felt awful for acting that way. Even though it was like listening to a story about someone else, Jenn's heart squeezed, and she drew a ragged breath. She didn't like that girl, not at all. "God," she whispered brokenly.

Braden's hand squeezed her shoulder. "You were young."

"Not much older now," Winona observed. "But maybe a bit wiser?"

Jenn didn't know. How could she know? Her fingers lifted to her necklace. "What about this?"

"Guess that's the only part of your inheritance you took. I remember Maria wearing it for a while, but it was Jeremiah's, from *his* father. Reckon you didn't think it was dirty like the money."

"Maybe." The blank wall remained even as the details were filled in.

Winona held out her coffee cup. Before Jenn could move, Braden went to refill it.

Finally, Jenn asked a question that seemed suddenly important. "What about my family? Who are they?"

"Good people, fairly young when they took you on right after Maria left. Sterling MacCallum is a police detective. Jessica, his wife, is a social worker. Sterling tried like hell to find you, but somehow you skipped without leaving any trace behind. They kept waiting for you to come home, sure you'd get over it, but you never did. They've been grieving over you for a long time now. Think you could find it in your heart to ease their sorrow, girl?"

"But I don't even remember them! How could I help them?"

"Seeing you and knowing you're alive would do most of the work. I can see you're a kind woman, and it might ease your heart some just to know them now. You need your own heart eased, too. You've been through a lot." Winona finished her coffee quickly then stood up. "These old bones need their bed."

Braden hurried to help her on with her coat. Winona paused at the door and looked back. "You think about it,

Jenny MacCallum. Even if you don't remember, you'll find something you need."

"I'll be back," Braden said as he followed her to the door.

She was still alone and without a real past. Rejected, kidnapped, adopted and a runaway. It was a hell of a résumé.

She wondered if she should just find a rock to crawl under. Because she really, really didn't want to be that girl. Unwanted. Then turning cruelly on those who had raised her.

No, she didn't like that person at all.

When Braden returned, to her surprise, he didn't say one thing about Winona's revelations. Instead, he swept her into her bed and made love to her, driving everything else from her mind.

But later, much later, she lay awake. The languor of lovemaking had long since departed. The arms around her felt good, but they didn't answer the fears that had plagued her and now plagued her even more.

She watched the faint movements of the firelight on the ceiling, trying to settle the revelations in her mind and heart.

But her heart didn't answer them. She might as well have read about Jennifer MacCallum in a novel. Hell, maybe she'd have connected more with a fictional character.

None of it felt as if it belonged to her, except the name Jennifer, a mountain, a Christmas pageant barely remembered. The world was probably full of Jennifers, though, so how could she be sure she was this one?

Her past gave her no answers. Her heart held no connections. They had been severed as if by a guillotine.

She needed to move. Nerves began to trouble her anew. Her fears had come to life, and now she had to deal with all this somehow.

And she really didn't want to be that selfish girl who had turned on and then run away from the people who had raised her. Who loved her.

Braden stirred then turned to gaze at her in the dim light. "Need to talk? Need to get up? You've become as stiff as a board."

She rose without a word and climbed into her warmest fleece sweatshirt and pants. Jamming her feet into quilted slippers, she walked over to the stove. But its warmth wouldn't reach her heart—she felt cold all the way through.

Braden joined her wearing only his jeans. He squatted to throw another log onto the fire then stepped back and faced her. "Want some coffee? Lights?"

"Coffee, please. No lights." She felt like a deck of cards that had been thrown into a fan, although the truth was, she'd felt that way before.

He started the coffee then sat at her feet, facing her. "Tough night," he remarked.

"Yeah." It had been, every bit of it. She just wished she knew how to deal with this, wish she didn't feel like shattered glass that she couldn't quite glue together.

"How did it make you feel?" he asked.

"Like I don't want to be that girl. That was my whole reaction. I don't remember any more than I did before, and I don't like that Jennifer MacCallum."

He nodded, but didn't say anything. Reaching up, he placed his hands on her curled-up legs and rubbed gently. When at long last he finally spoke, he said, "I think what matters is what Jennifer MacCallum does now. She was a young girl, really."

"I'm not much older."

"Maybe not in years, but certainly in experience."

She shook her head. "How can you like someone who turned on her adoptive parents that way? Who ran away? And since I can't remember a damn thing, how can I be sure I've learned anything at all?"

"Because you lost everything," he said simply. "Because you know better than anyone the price of running away, the cost of having no family, no roots."

"Yeah," she said almost bitterly. "I did the ultimate in running away."

"Not by choice, I suspect."

She shook her head a little, but despite her resistance, his words were rippling through her. Had she really learned something by her constant struggle to find her past? God, she hoped so.

He rose and poured coffee for both of them before settling again on the floor at her feet.

"You need sleep," she argued, trying to think of someone besides herself. "You must have a lot to do tomorrow."

"I've survived on short sleep before. I'm more worried about you."

"I'll be fine," she protested, although she wasn't really sure. Shattered glass, no way to put it back together again. Somehow she had to absorb all this and accept it.

"You've been fine on your own for some time now. Well, you're not alone anymore. You have friends and you have me. We're here for you."

It was a touching statement, but she wasn't quite ready to believe it. "What do *you* think of a girl who'd do that to her family?"

"You know, I was twenty-one not so long ago. I remember being pigheaded, stupid and very stubborn once

I'd made up my mind. I had the answers to everything. It's a wonder my family could put up with me. I went toe-to-toe with my father more than once. Hell, I can't even remember some of the things we fought about, but we fought. And my mother would always say, 'Bob, he's growing up. Trying to find his place. He'll settle down.'" He shrugged. "I think I gave my folks a harder time than all my brothers combined. Or maybe I was worse because I had all those older brothers. Sometimes I think I was kicking and screaming my way to maturity, or at least to getting them all to accept I wasn't just the baby anymore."

"It must have been hard." Not that she could really imagine it. She didn't have the experience from which to guess what it had been like. "But it sounds normal. What I did isn't."

"I don't know," he said. "Lots of young people run away from home. Unfortunately, too many of them never make it back."

She shook her head. "I was pretty old to pull that one."

"Not really. When the pressure gets to be too much, for whatever reason, any of us could decide to take a hike. Hell, Sutter moved to Seattle because of a big fight. It happens."

"But he didn't lose touch, and he came back."

A quiet sound escaped him. "You didn't *choose* to lose touch, remember? For all anyone knows, you might have been getting ready to head home when you were injured. Might have been only hours away from making a phone call. From the sound of it, you got your amnesia only a short time after you left."

"That's a pretty light to put it in."

"Well, it may be true. No way to know now."

Silence fell again, punctuated only by the faint crackling of the fire. Shadows danced on the walls, making it feel almost as if there were spirits in the room with them.

There was certainly a lot in the room with them. Whole bunches of unanswered questions, decisions to be made, a broken life that only seemed more broken now.

Finally, she put her coffee cup down on the table. "We both need some sleep."

"What are you going to do? Will you look for the MacCallums?"

"I don't know." She put her feet on the floor, and he stood. "I just don't know, Braden. They're strangers. I don't remember them. I feel no pull in that direction. What good would it do them to have a daughter who might as well be dead?"

"It might give them hope."

But he didn't say another word as he guided her back to the bed. This time they didn't make love. He pulled her back against him, spooning with her, holding her close as if he could keep everything at bay.

If only it were that easy.

Christmas was drawing close, and excitement filled the air. Most of it left Jenn untouched, but Vanessa was positively bubbling over about the opening of Maverick Manor, and telling everyone they were going to be amazed by the mural she had painted around the lobby, but she wouldn't share a single detail. "It's a surprise for everyone!" Jonah Dalton, her fiancé, merely smiled at her excitement but kept mum.

The whole town seemed to bustle with new life, and whether or not Jenn was as excited as everyone else didn't matter. She enjoyed watching the enthusiasm build, enjoyed watching the shoppers running around with secret treasures in their bags. She started spending more time at the donut shop, having coffee with her friends, or just sitting and watching life through the window.

She no longer felt such a strong need to be alone. She even, finally, confided to her friends about her amnesia.

They were sitting around the table at Callie Kennedy and Nate Crawford's place, jabbering about nothing consequential, when she dropped the bomb. She didn't know what kind of reaction she expected, but after a silence, she was suddenly awash in sympathy and questions. She felt surrounded by loving concern and hugs as the women promised to help her in any way they could. Then came the questions, mercifully truncated by Cecelia, whether she meant to or not.

"God, that must be awful," Mallory said. "How can you stand it?"

"Like she has any choice?" Callie remarked.

Vanessa remained silent longer than the rest. Finally, "Did you come here for a reason?"

"I've been trying to find something familiar," Jenn admitted. "Snow and mountains seemed to draw me."

"Well, you sure as hell found them," Cecelia said bluntly. "Seems like you found a cowboy, too."

Jenn flushed. "What do you mean?"

"Only that some folks have noticed that a certain Triple-T truck seems to make its way out to your place a lot."

The others giggled, seeming more interested by that than by the amnesia. While their reaction to her amnesia was a welcome relief, their interest in her relationship with Braden was not. Jenn smiled weakly, mainly because that truck hadn't been making its way to her very often. Braden called at least once a day, and they talked for hours sometimes, but he was buried in work, both the problems left by the storm, and his mother's insistence that it was time to deck out the Triple-T for the holidays. Apparently, she went whole hog.

Jenn thought of volunteering to help, but she was still feeling uncertain in so many ways. She didn't want to push herself on Braden and his family. Even without a memory, she understood that holidays to a great extent were purely a family affair. She wasn't part of the Traub family, even remotely. And she still didn't want to find a way to get in touch with the MacCallums. But she was missing Braden, and often wondered if he were trying to put distance between them. The excuses sounded real enough, and he *did* call a lot, but there was no escaping the sense that he didn't have a whole lot of time for her.

She told herself to buck up. He'd warned her he'd be busy at times. She couldn't expect him to show up every single day. But it was still hard to accept when she wanted him there all the time.

Five days before Christmas, Braden showed up at her place with a tree and all the trimmings.

"No home should be without one," he said as he edged through the door with cardboard boxes. "Now it's small, so it won't push you out, and it's artificial so you don't have to worry about dry needles, and do you need another wood delivery?"

"I was supposed to get a couple of cords last week. I don't know what happened."

"Well, that can wait until we put up this little old tree."

For the first time, the magic of the season began to really reach her. There was something about having her own tree, thanks to Braden, about setting it up and stringing the miniature lights, about opening the boxes of small but exquisite ornaments, that began to make her feel truly happy. Excited, even, almost like a kid. As if she could remember.

She brushed that thought away like an annoying gnat, and joined Braden's good humor as they worked on the tree. He often stood back to guide her as she went to hang an ornament, telling her whether to move it to the right or left.

"Are you an ornament perfectionist?" she finally demanded.

"You could say I was raised to be one. Not until the day we take the trees down will my mother stop adjusting them."

"Trees? Plural?"

"Sure. One for the family room, one for the living room, one for the dining room. She even has one in her and Dad's bedroom, but she doesn't let anyone else touch it."

"She must love Christmas."

"No question. It means having everyone home, a house full of family."

Jenn felt a pang of guilt as his words reminded her of a family that was missing all that because she had run away.

"Hey." Braden touched her chin and lifted her head. "No getting down. We were having fun."

The tree went into the corner between her sleep nook and the stove, protected from the heat of the woodstove by the dogleg in the wall. Braden moved the two armchairs a little so that they could sit and admire it.

"It's beautiful," she said. "I thought I could do without it, but I'm so glad it's here. Thank you."

"My pleasure." He paused. "I guess not having a bunch of good Christmas memories makes this a little meaningless to you."

"I'm enjoying everyone's excitement. People seem so happy. And I do have one Christmas memory, I think."

She told him about what had happened at the pageant, how she could feel herself dressed as an angel like Lily, and looking out into a sea of faces trying to see her parents. "I couldn't see them, though. At least not in my flashback."

"Well, that's something. Not much, I admit, but something. Maybe you'll get other flashes with time."

"Maybe." But now she wasn't sure she wanted them. Not given what she had done.

"Have you decided when you'll call them?" He didn't have to say who he meant. The MacCallums were hanging over her head like the Sword of Damocles.

"Not yet," she said, trying to sound firm. "I'm not ready yet."

"Ready for what?" he asked. "That they might be thrilled to see you and glad you're still alive?"

The tension came to a shrieking head then. "You can't know that! I don't know that. I did a terrible thing to them. What if they can't forgive me? Besides, they're strangers to me. God, wouldn't it be weird to have them call me their daughter when I don't even know who they are? What if I don't like them? What if they don't like me?"

"I somehow suspect they aren't like that. Winona said they looked everywhere for you. That they grieved."

"That doesn't mean anything. I was rejected before."

"What?" He rose to his feet, and the next thing she knew they were standing toe-to-toe, about to really get into it. A fight. Their first fight? Or their last one?

"My birth parents didn't want me, not either of them."

"But these people chose to adopt you!" His brow was lowering.

"And then I treated them like dirt. Why in the hell would they want anything to do with me ever again?"

"God!" he said exasperatedly. He ran his fingers through his hair. "Maybe you've forgotten the most important thing of all, Jenn."

"What's that?" she demanded.

"Love. What it really is." He swore and grabbed for his jacket. "Think about that, why don't you? You're judging people you can't remember, but what are you basing that judgment on? I thought you were braver than this."

"Braden…"

But he was already out the door, leaving ashes in his wake. Her mouth turned sour, and she felt as if her heart had been cleaved in two.

Maybe she *did* know something about love, because he had just cut her to ribbons.

Braden told himself to let go of it. It wasn't his problem, it was hers. She had to make the decision whether to reach out to her family. He reminded himself of her fear of the past, a fear that was probably even greater than her desire to know. He reminded himself that she didn't like the girl who had run away from her family. Why the hell would she want to know any more?

Of course he didn't think she was being fair to herself, but given her loss of memory, how could she even compare her actions to the actions of others her age? Hell, he'd even told her about Sutter, but that hadn't seemed to ease her guilt any.

It had been a really big deal when Sutter moved so far away after the blowup. Ellie had cried quite a bit, and Bob had got all stern-jawed. But Sutter hadn't stayed away. Once he'd found a way to make peace with the family—especially Forrest—he'd started coming home to visit. The important thing was, Sutter had not been lost forever.

Remembering his parting words to Jenn, however, he

felt pretty small. That had been a terribly cutting thing to say, yet it went to the heart of his own fear: that she might not be capable of really forming a relationship. No past, no memories—it would be easy to imagine her turning into a rolling stone, always looking for something that would never be there.

Of course that concerned him, because he had come to care about her a whole lot. His inability to imagine life without Jenn had grown by leaps and bounds until he was cussing the demands of his own life, demands he had always welcomed until they kept him from seeing Jenn as often as he would have liked.

It seemed the bug had bit him, and it had bit him with no guarantees of any kind.

Then, finally, he realized he'd had enough. This had to be settled somehow. If Jenn hated him forever, then so be it. At least he'd understand where he stood with her.

Not his business? Hell, yeah, it was his business because he was involved. And it really bothered him that she wouldn't make one blessed phone call to put some peoples' minds and hearts to rest.

Maybe it would turn out bad. Maybe nothing would come of it, but there were a couple of parents who had a right to know that their daughter wasn't dead.

Remembering all too well his mother's grief after Sutter had left, he knew something about that end of it. As for Jenn, she needed the closure of knowing, whether she wanted to admit it or not.

That night, instead of calling Jenn, he hunted for a phone number in Whitehorn. To his relief, the MacCallums were still listed there.

A short while later, a woman's voice answered the phone.

"Hello?"

"Jessica MacCallum?"

"Yes."

"You don't know me, Mrs. MacCallum. My name is Braden Traub. I'm a rancher over in Rust Creek Falls."

"I recognize the Traub name," she said warmly. "Would you rather talk to my husband? At least, I'm assuming this is business of some kind."

"I can talk to you, but you'd better sit down."

"Why?"

"Because I know your daughter Jennifer. She's alive, and she has amnesia."

When he hung up the phone a half hour later, he wondered if he'd go to hell forever.

Chapter Eleven

The Maverick Manor's grand opening hovered only one day away. Vanessa was in a flutter, nerves and excitement keeping her high. All her work in decorating the place was going to be on display, and she both feared and craved the reactions. She must have called Jenn a dozen times, and probably called their other girlfriends, as well.

The entire town had been invited for the grand opening Christmas party, which promised plenty of food and drink from the Traub family's own relative, Thunder Canyon cousin DJ Traub and his popular barbecue restaurant, DJ's Rib Shack, as well as the first peek at the work that had been going on for months. It would be a milestone for the town, especially after the flood had taken so much.

During one excited call, Vanessa reminded her, "Don't forget to dress up. An excuse to dress up is rare enough around here."

"I bought a dress," Jenn assured her. "Just for this." It had seemed like a terrible extravagance, but important anyway. She just hoped her legs wouldn't freeze, because even though the weather had remained clear since the blizzard, it didn't seem to have warmed much.

Braden said he'd meet her there. He hadn't come by since their fight, and he hadn't come over, or even suggested it. Now he wasn't even going to take her to the grand opening, but rather meet her there. That sounded entirely too casual to soothe her aching heart.

She missed him. She missed him intensely, and feared she'd driven him away forever. Why couldn't he understand the tangle of feelings she had over the MacCallums? It wasn't as if she could remember them. Just thinking about reaching out to them made her throat lock up and her mouth grow dry with fear. She didn't know which would be worse, being rejected by them for her behavior—behavior she couldn't even remember but sounded pretty bad to her—or being welcomed like the prodigal daughter. Either way, they were strangers, and she couldn't imagine how she would handle it.

Well, she told herself, she had time to think about it. First she had a party to get ready for.

In the late afternoon, the day before the big bash, the phone rang again. Jenn expected it to be Vanessa once more. Even Jonah's calming words weren't helping much with her friend's nerves. Busy as she was with last-minute details, she seemed to need frequent breaks on the phone for reassurance.

Smiling, Jenn answered, glad that she could provide even some small comfort to Vanessa.

Instead, for only the second time since he'd brought the Christmas tree, she heard Braden's voice.

"Hi, Jenn," he said quietly.

"I thought you were mad at me."

"I wasn't, not really. Just a little disturbed. I'm sorry. I've been thinking of you constantly."

"I have, too," she admitted. Even though it had only been two days, they had been the longest two days of her life, feeling like forever.

"Would you mind if I came over?"

"Of course not." She was past playing hard to get, if she'd ever been capable of it.

"Would it be all right if I bring a couple of friends?"

She looked around the cabin. "I'm not exactly set up for entertaining."

"They want to meet you. I'd like that, too. Don't worry, we'll manage. Just put the coffee on."

Wondering what the heck he was doing, she started the coffee and looked around for where she had left the coffee cake she had bought that morning at the bakery. The whole darn town looked so festive right now that she kept having urges to splurge a little on something special.

At least she had clean dishes. Between phone calls from Vanessa, she'd spent a whole lot of needless time tidying this space up, trying to keep busy and ease her anxiety over, well, over everything. Braden's parting shot, what it meant, the unknown family hanging over her head. Her lack of a past. Everything seemed to be coming to a head at once. Maybe if she were honest, she'd admit she was almost as nervous as Vanessa, Nate and Jonah were, though her fears weren't as imminent. So much depended on the success of the Manor.

But Braden's call, the fact that he was coming over to see her again, leavened her mood and eased her doubts. Maybe one thing in her life would work right. Maybe Braden wouldn't abandon her.

Although in honest moments she couldn't imagine why he'd want to hang around someone as messed up as she was.

At last she heard the sound of his truck and another vehicle. The idea of meeting some of his friends made her hold back rather than race to the door. She didn't want to appear too eager in front of strangers.

She heard voices outside. One of them sounded like

a woman. She couldn't explain why that surprised her. When he'd said friends, for some reason she had assumed it would be a couple of guys.

Then Braden threw the door open without knocking, and an attractive, middle-aged couple stepped in. She wondered if they were his relatives from out of town or something. The woman appeared to be in her late forties or early fifties, with dark hair that was beginning to silver. The man could only have been a couple of years older, but gray had totally taken over his temples. Their gazes swept the cabin swiftly, then fell on her.

In the next instant, Jenn's world turned upside down.

"Oh, my God," said the woman. "Jenny!" Tears started rolling down her face. The man with her quickly put his arm around her shoulders, but his eyes remained on Jenn, seeming to devour her. "Jennifer," he said, echoing the woman.

Jenn looked at Braden, even though she somehow already knew. Her legs began to feel like rubber bands, and it was a good thing the chair was right beside her. She collapsed on it, unable to speak. Part of her tried to summon some fury that he'd done this to her, but the fury wouldn't come. She sat trembling, looking at a weeping woman and a man with a kind, worn face.

"Jenn," Braden said, clearing his throat. "I'd like you to meet Jessica and Sterling MacCallum."

Braden took over. Jenn was incapable of moving, of responding. She didn't recognize these people, and her heart felt almost crushed that she couldn't. Strangers who were not strangers. This wasn't right. Everything was out of kilter, off balance.

But Braden ushered Jessica to the other armchair then brought the chairs from the dinette for himself and Sterling. Nobody seemed to know what to say for several minutes, but the tears kept rolling down Jessica's face.

Braden brought coffee that no one even touched. Then he sat waiting, as they were all waiting for whatever might come.

It was Jessica, finally, who broke the silence. "I know," she said brokenly, "that you don't remember us. Braden told us about your amnesia. I don't want to overwhelm you in any way, but sweet Lord, I am so happy to see you alive!"

Faced with these people, Jenn took her courage into her hands and asked the question that had been terrifying her since Winona had told her the truth. "You don't hate me?"

"Why in the world would we do that?" Sterling asked, his voice gravelly with emotion.

"I hear I was awful to you before I left."

He waved a hand. "We've been worried, we've been scared, and finally we thought we'd lost you for good. That you were dead. We didn't even have a grave to put flowers on. All we wanted in this world was to have our daughter back."

Something inside Jenn began to thaw. The wall that fear had built began to melt away. "I'm sorry I don't remember you. I'm sorry I ran away like that."

Jessica pulled a wad of tissues from her purse and wiped at her tears. "None of that matters. We'll deal with it. The important thing is that you're still alive. If you never remember us, at least we have that. You're alive."

Jenn looked at Braden, as if he might have some answer to this strange situation, but he was simply smiling faintly, silent and staying out of this. He'd made it happen. Surely he should have something to say for himself. But he didn't.

Which left her. The MacCallums seemed uncertain how to proceed. Well, of course they would. She didn't remember them. They were probably on tenterhooks, too.

Jenn struggled for something positive to say, something encouraging, but she kept coming up against her inability to remember these people. Her parents, it seemed.

So she fell back on the only thing she knew for certain. "I was trying to get back home," she said slowly. "I know that much. It's been driving me for four years. But I feel so bad that I can't remember you. I admit I was afraid, too. Afraid of not knowing you and the kind of people you are, afraid of how you'd react to me. And honestly, I don't like the few things I learned about myself from Winona. So I was afraid of the things I'd learn about myself. I guess I said terrible things to you, and I can't even really apologize because I don't remember!"

Sterling leaned forward, resting his elbows on his knees. "Forget what Winona told you. That old busybody has only part of the story."

"Yes," Jessica said. Her tears had begun to dry, but she couldn't drag her gaze from Jenn. "She couldn't possibly know it all. We made some mistakes, too."

Jenn looked between the MacCallums wishing she could feel even the faintest spark of recognition. Just one little quiver. "You made mistakes?"

"We've had plenty of time to think about it," Sterling said. "You were a young woman, and instead of pressing you to accept an inheritance you felt was filthy, we should have let you decide. You weren't our little girl anymore. Sure, we wanted you to have a secure future, but really, it wasn't our decision. So instead of letting you do as you chose, we fought with you. I'm not surprised you felt you had to get away."

Jenn felt a stirring of warmth toward him. He was apologizing to her. Whether it was justified, she didn't know, but he was trying to mend the fence from his side.

"I don't remember," she said finally. It was her only answer.

Jessica surprised her by rising from her chair and coming to drop a kiss on her head. "You don't have to remember. We'll fill in the gaps for you. Show you all the photos. Tell you how much we've always loved you. And you still don't have to remember. Just share your future with us as much as you comfortably can. We couldn't bear to lose you again."

Jessica returned to her seat. Jenn felt all jumbled up inside. Her fear was gone for the first time in forever, and she knew she should be feeling happy to have found her place, if not her memory. But the lack of memory had never been starker than it was right now. She was sitting and talking with her parents, and they might as well have been strangers. Nice strangers, but still.

She glanced at Braden and wondered what he was thinking, but still nothing showed on his face except a faint smile. She supposed she should be angry with him for overriding her desire to wait, but she couldn't manage it. He had saved her days, weeks or even months of agonizing over whether to call these people. For good or ill, it was done.

"I'm sorry," she said again, looking at Jessica and then Sterling. "I wish I could remember you. I feel awful that I can't."

Sterling shook his head. "Let go of that. We're just glad to see you again. It's time to start building bridges.

You might never remember, but the important thing is what we do now. We want you to come home with us."

Braden stood. That was his cue, he supposed. He had seen the fear leak out of Jenn, but he couldn't do anything about the rest of it. She would have to deal with this however she could, as best she could. Going home with her parents seemed like the right thing to do, even though it would take her away from him. He wouldn't deny her the opportunity to build a relationship with them, perhaps have her memory jarred a bit so that she could remember some of her past. Not for anything would he deny her the chance, even if it meant he would never see her again.

Watching the fear go, watching Jessica and Sterling reach out to her, watching the dawn of small hopes in her expression…that was all he needed.

"I need to run," he said, when Sterling and Jessica paused in the midst of recalling Jenn's childhood, recollections that were making Jenn smile and relax even more. "Still some stuff to do tonight."

He wouldn't have been surprised if Jenn had merely nodded and let him go with a simple good-night. He was well aware that she had every right to be mad at him for taking charge and putting her in this position without warning.

But instead, she followed him to the door, and after he pulled his jacket on, she laid her hand on his arm.

He looked at her, sensing she wanted to say something, but he couldn't tell what it was, and this might not even be the right time. Not with the MacCallums here. If she wanted to rake him over the coals, best she did it when they weren't around to be hurt.

He bent, and tried to speak volumes with a necessarily brief and chaste kiss. "Tomorrow night?" he asked. "Meet at the shindig?"

She nodded. "Absolutely." Then she smiled.

He carried that smile away with him, tucked in his heart. After tomorrow night, he might not see it again for a long while. She might well transplant herself permanently to Whitehorn, and construct her life there where at least she would have the MacCallums' support.

He stepped out into the night, closing the door behind him, and sucked in deep drafts of icy air. He might have just closed a huge door, he realized. A much more important one than the door of her cabin. He might have just helped Jenn leave for good.

The thought squeezed his heart like a giant fist, telling him how much and how rapidly he had come to care for this young woman. He'd closed doors like this one before, but it had never hurt so much.

Damn!

Small comfort that he believed he had done what was right for Jenn. A lot of her questions could now be answered. Even if she never got her memory back, she'd have answers for those questions she was always trying to evade. She'd have that sense of continuity that had been interrupted, even though he supposed it might never be the same for her as for everyone else.

The drive home was at once contradictorily long and too short. He wasn't ready to join the holiday cheer, and while his whole family was gathered in the main house, sleeping in their old bedrooms with their wives and fiancees, kids sprawled in sleeping bags in the family room, reliving past holidays and good memories while building new ones, he just didn't have the heart for it tonight.

Instead, he drove past the house out to his own little place, an unnecessary house, given that he'd always have room with his parents, except that a few years ago he'd felt a need to have his own space, his own place.

Which he guessed wasn't so very different with Jenn. He'd built a house. Now she would build a past of sorts. A place of her own in a world that had been too blank for long.

He ought to be celebrating for her. Instead, once he was inside, he built a fire and poured himself a whiskey. Sitting there alone, away from everyone he cared about, he had some small sense of the isolation Jenn had endured, except hers hadn't been by choice.

He'd built this place partly with an eye to a future that would include a wife and maybe a couple of kids. A place of their own.

Not likely he could deprive Jenn of her family. He could only wonder at himself. The unsnaggable bachelor who had broken off every relationship early. For good reasons, or so he had thought when he did it. Jenn was different. He couldn't understand it any other way. Some ineffable quality of hers had drawn him and snared his heart.

Just in time for him to wave it all goodbye.

Hell, he thought, and poured another whiskey. He'd done it to himself this time.

Jenn walked through the next day in a daze. She met her parents for breakfast in town, and they'd talked for hours. Well, Jessica and Sterling had. She'd mostly listened, drinking it in, trying to create associations in the empty places of her memory.

More than once, they pressed her to come home with them. More than once she simply said, "Not yet."

"But we want you for Christmas," Jessica finally said.

Jenn was almost appalled at herself when she answered, "Not until after Christmas. Please understand. The people I know, my friends, they're here. I want to be with them. After Christmas, okay?"

They looked saddened, but they accepted it. Eventually, Jessica brightened. "We'll have a late Christmas with you. Big dinner and all of that. Better late than..."

She didn't say the word never. Of course she couldn't since she and Sterling had concluded a while back that Jennifer must be dead.

Sterling surprised her by clasping her hand warmly. "Call us when you're ready. We'll be waiting. As long as you want."

Jenn waved them on their way then headed back to her cabin. Hard to believe it was after noon already, and the big shindig started at five. She needed to wash her hair, maybe style it a bit if she could remember how. Ponytails didn't seem right for tonight.

And then, of course, there were Vanessa's calls. Her nervousness practically shrieked over the phone. Jenn lost track of how many times she said, "It's going to be great! It's going to be perfect!"

Five o'clock seemed to roll around awfully fast for Jenn. Wearing her new dress, a deep blue velvet with threads of gold in it, her hair styled up into some kind of bun, her tarnished necklace around her neck, she headed for the lodge just outside town.

The parking lot was full of cars, the elaborately redesigned entryway full of people. It seemed everyone from Rust Creek Falls, Thunder Canyon and even as far as Kalispell wanted to be here tonight. Jenn had some trouble finding a place to park, then she joined the moving throngs all headed for the Maverick Manor.

She hadn't been here for the Great Flood, but she had

already learned that this opening was a milestone event in most minds. While there was still plenty of recovery underway, this was a big one. It meant there would be tourist business, or so everyone hoped.

She wasn't sure how much good that would do for this small, rustic town in the long run, but folks were happy, and she wished Nate Crawford well in his enterprise. He seemed like an okay guy. And then there was Vanessa, who had been pouring her heart and soul into the mural that would be revealed tonight, and Jonah who must be tied up in knots because he'd helped with some of the redesign of the place.

She barely got in the door before Vanessa grabbed her. "Tell me it's okay."

"I haven't had a chance to see it yet," Jenn protested, amused. "Do you want me to just say yes, or would you rather I look first and tell you the truth?"

Vanessa rolled her eyes. "Don't do this to me."

"Let me walk around. Give me a few minutes to look. I'm sure it's perfect."

It was not at all what Jenn expected, though. She began to move through the growing crowd and look at the huge walls. Vanessa seemed to have painted the history of the area, of the ranchers of Whitehorn and Rumor, the Queen of Hearts Mine of Thunder Canyon—and even a tip of the hat to Lily Divine, the once-notorious "Shady Lady" of that still-booming mountain town. The mural also portrayed the more recent history of Rust Creek Falls. As she began to recognize some of the families portrayed up there, from the Crawfords, Daltons, Traubs and others, shown doing what they did for a living, she felt her amazement grow.

Over there, tucked in a corner, she saw the Newcomers Club, all those smiling faces of people who had become her friends. She could even pick out her own face, though it was in the background. As if Vanessa had sensed she was hiding.

She loved it. She turned again and again and realized that Vanessa had given this town a beautiful gift: she had given it its memory. It was enough to make her eyes prickle.

"Well?" Vanessa said impatiently from behind her.

Jenn whirled and threw her arms around her. "Fabulous. Perfect. Maybe it means more to me, I don't know."

Vanessa stepped back, raising a brow. "Why would it mean more to you?"

"Because this is the town's continuity," Jenn said, waving her arm. "Its history. Its memory. Maybe most people don't know how much that means."

But the comments from everywhere were approving, and Jenn could hear them as Vanessa grabbed her again for another hug. "I love you, girl."

"Hey," said a deep male voice, "that's my line."

Jenn's heart stopped. Turning from Vanessa, she saw Braden, all duded up in a suit and string tie. She wanted to throw herself at him but held back because it was possible he was trying to ease her out of his life. He smiled at her, but it was an awkward smile, only raising her fears.

"I have only one criticism," he said to Vanessa.

"What's that, cowboy?"

"You put the Traubs and Crawfords too close together."

Vanessa started laughing. "Work it out, you bunch of stubborn idiots." Then, still grinning, she let Jonah draw her away to the groaning buffet tables.

Braden stepped closer. "How are you?"

"Never better," Jenn answered not quite truthfully. The one thing that could have made her feel better was if Braden had at least hugged her. Even given her a little hello kiss.

"So you're not mad at me over the MacCallums?"

"No. I guess I could have been, but I'm just so glad to be over that hump. They're wonderful people." She looked around. "Is your family here?"

"Everyone's here, but finding someone in this crush is almost impossible. So are you going home with the MacCallums?"

Jenn turned her gaze back to him. "Not until after Christmas."

"I'm surprised."

"Why?"

"I figured now that you had a family, you'd want to go with them. Find your old life. No reason to commit to hanging around here anymore."

Jenn's jaw dropped. "Braden?"

He threw up a hand. "I'm making a hash out of this, and I can hardly hear myself think. Want something to eat?"

"No!" Frustration surged in her. "Are you telling me to get lost?"

His eyes widened, then a change came over him. His jaw set, and he grabbed her elbow. "Did I tell you how beautiful you look tonight?"

"You overlooked that part," she said acidly.

"Well, you do. Where in the hell is your coat?"

"Checked at the coat check with a million others. What…"

"Hell," he said. He'd been headed for the lobby doors but took a sudden sharp turn toward a closed door near the front of the lobby.

"Where are you quit dragging me?"

"I'm trying to find a quiet place."

"Good luck."

But somehow he managed it. Leading her through a door labeled "Employees Only" they entered a silent hallway with empty open offices on either side. He pulled her into one of them and closed the door.

"What's going on?" she demanded.

"I'm acting like a caveman."

"I can see that. But why?"

"Because…because I've spent the past two days thinking about you going to Whitehorn. And you're going. It's not exactly a hop-skip away. You'll be there, and I'll be here, and I won't get to see you very often."

"I'm not going forever," she protested. It was nice, though, to know he cared that she'd be leaving. She'd begun to wonder. But she just didn't know how to reassure him. If he even wanted reassurance.

"Maybe you don't think you're going forever," he said. "Maybe you don't intend to. But that could change. You might find everything you want there."

Not him, she thought. She wouldn't find Braden there. A terrible heaviness began to settle in her heart.

"Anyway," he continued before she could respond, "I've got to face facts. You've got a future waiting for you, one that gives you at least some of your past. I don't want to stand in your way, and I sure as hell can't ask you for any kind of commitment. Not under these circumstances."

She'd been in pretty much of a daze since the arrival of the MacCallums, with an overload of things to absorb. But all of a sudden matters began to clear up. She focused intently on one word as her heart began to race. "Commitment? What kind of commitment?"

"This isn't very romantic, is it."

A flare of annoyance sparked in her. "Will you stop being so evasive? What exactly do you mean?"

He sighed then released her arm and took her hands. "I don't have any practice at this. I've never said anything like this before. But I want to be fair to you."

"So be fair by telling me what you're driving at." Hope and fear warred within her, familiar even now, but different. This wasn't about amnesia. This was about what she truly wanted *now*.

"I love you," he said finally. "I can't escape it, and since I brought the MacCallums into your life, I've been staring down a bleak road without you. I know that you need to go, but I don't want to let you go. Selfish, but there it is. I want you in my life forever. I want you to marry me. But you can't make that decision now."

Surprise filled her, even as joy began to wash away the fear. "I can't? Who says I can't? Nothing has affected my ability to know how I feel."

He squeezed her hand, and the expression of hope on his face was almost painful. "Do you think…you can love me?"

Her heart cracked wide open. "Braden, I already do. With my whole being. I thought you were trying to say goodbye to me."

"Never!" His eyes blazed, and he pulled her into his arms, holding her so tightly she could barely breathe, kissing her as if she were the breath of life itself. When he dragged his mouth from hers, he said raggedly, "You don't have to promise anything. Not yet. Your family…"

"They're nice people. I want to get to know them better. I'm going to visit them, but it's just a visit, because there's only one place on earth I want to be. With you."

He hugged her for a long, long time, his face pressed to her neck. She hugged him back, never wanting to let go.

But finally he eased his hold. "We're being rude to our friends, I guess. Time to get out there and ooh and aah appropriately. Later?"

"Yes, later."

It was likely, she thought as they returned to the lobby hand in hand, that anyone who looked at them would know the truth. That only made her smile wider.

Braden loved her. Who needed more than that?

Epilogue

Christmas morning dawned clear, bright and cold. Jenn stood at the window, squinting out at the winter beauty, wrapped in her warmest robe and slippers.

Strong arms closed around her from behind. "These have been the best two days of my life," Braden said.

"I'm pretty sure I can say the same." She turned within the circle of his arms, smiling, to look at him.

"Merry Christmas, love."

"Merry Christmas," she answered. "I'm sorry I don't have a gift for you, but time got away from me." She didn't mention the uncertainty that had nearly paralyzed her. That now seemed like part of a distant past. Braden had made sure that she knew how much he wanted her.

"You're the only gift I want. I'd love to be giving you an engagement ring this morning, but I want you to pick it out."

"Oh, Braden…" She leaned against him, pressing her cheek to his shoulder, filled with inexpressible gratitude. She had lost a lot, but she had found the most priceless gift of all. "So little seems to matter anymore except that we're together. I love you with my whole heart."

"I love you, too, sweetheart. I'm bursting with it." Then he sighed. "Unfortunately, it's time to head out to the Triple-T."

She lifted her head. "Already?"

"Big brunch to be followed by huge dinner later." He tipped her chin a little higher and searched her eyes. "Are you ready for this? The whole clan can be overwhelming, but I promise not to leave your side."

Her fear of large groups hadn't entirely abandoned her, but she figured she needed to do this, needed to overcome her resistance.

"We don't have to go," he said. "If you want, I'll give them a call and…"

"No." She pressed her fingertips to his lips. "I've been invited to join the Traub family for Christmas. That's not an invitation I want to turn down. Ever."

He smiled softly, his eyes filled with warmth. "You are so brave. Have I told you that?"

"Once or twice, I think."

"Well, I'll keep telling you. Brave. Resourceful. Smart. Beautiful. An incredible lover. A marvelous companion…"

"Oh, stop," she interrupted, her cheeks flaming. "I'm not perfect."

"In every way that counts." Then he lifted her off her feet and swung her in a circle. "Welcome to my life, Jennifer MacCallum. There's been a place waiting for you in my heart since I was born."

Love had rescued her, and now joy swept her into a whole new world, a world with family, friends, and everything she had ever lacked.

Her search for her memory had brought her a future brighter than any she had ever dreamed. Who would have believed she could be so lucky?

A couple of hours later, when she stood amidst the warm and welcoming Traub family, and applause greeted

Braden's announcement of their engagement, followed by more hugs than she could count, she knew she had truly found her home. She belonged at last.

* * * * *

#2377 NEVER TRUST A COWBOY • by Kathleen Eagle
Who's the cowboy on her doorstep? Lila Flynn wonders. The ranch hand who shows up looking for a job is a mystery—and a charmer! Handsome Delano Fox is a man of many talents *and* secrets, and he soon makes himself indispensable on Lila's South Dakota ranch. But can he heal the beauty's wounded heart—without betraying her trust?

#2378 A ROYAL FORTUNE
The Fortunes of Texas: Cowboy Country • by Judy Duarte
Proper British noble Jensen Fortune Chesterfield isn't looking for a lady of the manor...until he gets lassoed by the love of a lifetime! While visiting family in tiny Horseback Hollow, Texas, Jensen falls head-over-Oxfords for quirky cowgirl Amber Jones. They are two complete opposites, but their mutual attraction is undeniable. But can Jensen and Amber ever come together—for better *and* for worse?

#2379 THE HOMECOMING QUEEN GETS HER MAN
The Barlow Brothers • by Shirley Jump
When former beauty queen Meri Prescott returns home to Stone Gap, North Carolina, to care for her grandfather, she's not the same girl she was when she left. Her physical and emotional scars mark her as different—like her ex, former soldier Jack Barlow. He suffers from PTSD after his best friend's death. Can Meri and Jack heal each other's wounds to create a future together?

#2380 CLAIMING HIS BROTHER'S BABY • by Helen Lacey
Horse rancher Tanner McCord returned home to Crystal Point, Australia, to settle his brother's estate...not to fall in love with the woman who'd borne his brother's son. Beautiful Cassie Duncan is focused on her baby, Oliver, but can't resist her boy's loner uncle. As Tanner steps in to care for his newfound family, he might just find his very own happily-ever-after!

#2381 ROMANCING THE RANCHER
The Pirelli Brothers • by Stacy Connelly
Jarrett Deeks knows about healing a horse's broken spirit, but little does the rugged rancher realize that an injured nurse, Theresa Pirelli, will end up mending his broken heart! Theresa is used to curing patients, not being one. But Jarrett's tender bedside manner makes her think twice about returning to her busy life once she is recovered...and staying with him forever.

#2382 FINDING HIS LONE STAR LOVE • by Amy Woods
Manager at a Texas observatory, Lucy keeps her head out of the stars. She's focused on her niece, Shiloh, for whom she is a guardian. Her world is thrown out of orbit when handsome Sam Haynes shows up in town. Sam just found out Shiloh is his long-lost daughter, but he's kept it secret. As he falls for lovely Lucy and sweet Shiloh, can the chef cook up a delicious future for them all?

REQUEST YOUR FREE BOOKS!
2 FREE NOVELS PLUS 2 FREE GIFTS!

⟨H⟩HARLEQUIN

SPECIAL EDITION
Life, Love & Family

YES! Please send me 2 FREE Harlequin® Special Edition novels and my 2 FREE gifts (gifts are worth about $10). After receiving them, if I don't wish to receive any more books, I can return the shipping statement marked "cancel." If I don't cancel, I will receive 6 brand-new novels every month and be billed just $4.74 per book in the U.S. or $5.24 per book in Canada. That's a savings of at least 14% off the cover price! It's quite a bargain! Shipping and handling is just 50¢ per book in the U.S. and 75¢ per book in Canada.* I understand that accepting the 2 free books and gifts places me under no obligation to buy anything. I can always return a shipment and cancel at any time. Even if I never buy another book, the two free books and gifts are mine to keep forever.

235/335 HDN F45Y

Name _____ (PLEASE PRINT)

Address _____ Apt. #

City _____ State/Prov. _____ Zip/Postal Code

Signature (if under 18, a parent or guardian must sign)

Mail to the **Harlequin® Reader Service:**
IN U.S.A.: P.O. Box 1867, Buffalo, NY 14240-1867
IN CANADA: P.O. Box 609, Fort Erie, Ontario L2A 5X3

Want to try two free books from another line?
Call 1-800-873-8635 or visit www.ReaderService.com.

* Terms and prices subject to change without notice. Prices do not include applicable taxes. Sales tax applicable in N.Y. Canadian residents will be charged applicable taxes. Offer not valid in Quebec. This offer is limited to one order per household. Not valid for current subscribers to Harlequin Special Edition books. All orders subject to credit approval. Credit or debit balances in a customer's account(s) may be offset by any other outstanding balance owed by or to the customer. Please allow 4 to 6 weeks for delivery. Offer available while quantities last.

Your Privacy—The Harlequin® Reader Service is committed to protecting your privacy. Our Privacy Policy is available online at www.ReaderService.com or upon request from the Harlequin Reader Service.

We make a portion of our mailing list available to reputable third parties that offer products we believe may interest you. If you prefer that we not exchange your name with third parties, or if you wish to clarify or modify your communication preferences, please visit us at www.ReaderService.com/consumerschoice or write to us at Harlequin Reader Service Preference Service, P.O. Box 9062, Buffalo, NY 14269. Include your complete name and address.

HSE13R

SPECIAL EXCERPT FROM

♦ **HARLEQUIN**

SPECIAL EDITION

*Jensen Fortune Chesterfield is only in
Horseback Hollow, Texas, to see his new niece...not
get lassoed by a cowgirl! Amber Rogers isn't the kind
of woman Jensen ever imagined falling for. But, as
Amber's warm heart and outgoing ways melt his heart,
the handsome aristocrat begins to wonder if he might
find true love on the range after all...*

***

"What...was...that...kiss?" She stopped, her words coming out in raspy little gasps.

"...all about?" he finished for her.

She merely nodded.

"I don't know. It just seemed like an easier thing to do than to talk about it."

Maybe so, but being with Jensen was still pretty clandestine, what with meeting in the shadows, under the cloak of darkness.

The British Royal and the Cowgirl. They might be attracted to each other—and she might be good enough for him to entertain the idea of a few kisses in private or even a brief, heated affair. And maybe she ought to consider the same thing for herself, too.

But it would never last. Especially if the press—or the town gossips—got wind of it.

So she shook it all off—the secretive nature of it all, as well as the sparks and the chemistry, and opened the passenger door. "Good night, Jensen."

"What about dinner?" he asked. "I still owe you, remember?"

Yep, she remembered. Trouble was, she was afraid if she got in any deeper with him, there'd be a lot she'd have a hard time forgetting.

"We'll talk about it later," she said.

"Tomorrow?"

"Sure. Why not?"

"I may have to take my brother and sister to the airport, although I'm not sure when. I'll have to find out. Maybe we can set something up after I get home."

"Maybe so." She wasn't going to count on it, though. Especially when she had the feeling he wouldn't want to be seen out in public with her—where the newshounds or local gossips might spot them.

But as she headed for her car, she wondered if, when he set his mind on something, he might be as persistent as those pesky reporters he tried to avoid.

Well, Amber Rogers was no pushover. And if Jensen Fortune Chesterfield thought he'd met someone different from his usual fare, he didn't know the half of it. Because he'd more than met his match.

***

We hope you enjoyed this sneak peek at
A ROYAL FORTUNE by USA TODAY bestselling
author Judy Duarte, the first book in the brand-new
Harlequin® Special Edition continuity
THE FORTUNES OF TEXAS:
COWBOY COUNTRY!

On sale in January 2015, wherever
Harlequin Special Edition books and ebooks are sold.

HARLEQUIN®

A *Romance* FOR EVERY MOOD™

JUST CAN'T GET ENOUGH?

Join our social communities
and talk to us online.

You will have access to the latest
news on upcoming titles and special
promotions, but most importantly,
you can talk to other fans about your
favorite Harlequin reads.

Harlequin.com/Community

f Facebook.com/HarlequinBooks

Twitter.com/HarlequinBooks

P Pinterest.com/HarlequinBooks